Spider Moth

Contemporary Cryptids

Amara Lynn

Published by Amara Lynn, 2023.

SPIDER MOTH

First edition. November 21, 2023.

ISBN: 979-8223567165

Written by Amara Lynn.

Table of Contents

Author's Note:

The work referenced within is used in parody of the source material, or to critique, comment, or make jokes. The author does not own any rights to the referenced source material.

All places referenced within are used fictitiously. Any resemblance to people (or cryptids), living or nonliving, is coincidental. Cryptids (probably) aren't real, and it isn't recommended to move across the country or go into the woods searching for one to get your jollies on.

To all the Twilight fans who are now queer and monsterfucker lovers.

Chapter One

Forks

In the state of Washington, under a near constant cover of clouds and rain, there is a small town named Forks. Population: 3,295 people. This is where I'm moving.

I've always wanted to say that. I'm not Bella Swan, though. I'm a guy, who thought he was a confused girl at one point when I had a crush on not only Edward and Jacob, but Bella and Alice. And Rosalie. And Jasper. I was like Bella on that first day in the cafeteria: bi as hell and didn't know who I found the most attractive. Other than that, I'm nothing like Bella, except for the fact that I'm moving to Forks.

I'm not moving to Forks to be with my dad while my mom is on the roads with her new husband, I'm not from Arizona, and in fact I hate the heat and the sun. I'd rather have darkness and the fluorescent glow of a lamp in my arms any day.

So, why am I moving to Forks? For work, naturally. Literally. I work with nature, forestry. Okay, yes, it's also kinda my dream, as a closet Twilight fan. But I do study forestry. And while I don't expect to find a secret group of werewolves or a coven of vampires out here, I am curious if other cryptids exist.

That's what I'm here to find out. While studying regular plants and wildlife.

When I arrive in Forks, I have to take a cab to my new apartment. My rickety old car (no, it wasn't a red truck) wouldn't have made it cross country, so I plan to get another car here. The old one is safe in the care of my younger sister, Jezz.

Speaking of, my phone buzzes in the cab.

When I pick up, I'm immediately bombarded, without even saying hello.

"Did you make it okay? I assume your plane didn't crash if you picked up? Right? Are you at your apartment yet?" Jezz says all of this without taking a breath.

"Yes, no, it didn't, no. I'm in a cab."

She lets out a heavy breath. "You will call me if you need anything or have a life threatening incident, right?"

"Yes, I will."

I'm very aware of the fact that traditionally, one would expect the older sibling to look after the younger one. That would be logical if I weren't a fucking klutz. Years of me falling on my ass or getting hit in the head with random objects have led Jezz to be the more protective one.

"Okay, good. Make sure you don't trip or anything getting into your apartment."

"Way to fucking jinx a guy, Jezz."

"Oops! Sorry!" I can hear the clap of her hand over her mouth.

"I'll talk to you later."

"Okay, bye!"

I don't know how she manages to be overbearing and flighty at the same time.

When I finally get to my apartment, which is a basic, dinky thing, I haul my measly two suitcases in and sprawl on the floor. My furniture isn't here yet. For now I just want to stare into the void of my ceiling and be a fucking blob.

I text Jezz to say I'm in my apartment and send her a picture of the ceiling for shits and giggles.

It took me like, ten years, but I'm here. Finally I'm in Forks. I'm glad to be far away from middle of fucking nowhere Ohio, and its neighbor, West Virginia, Mothman country. Maybe here in this chosen exile, I can forget about all things mothpeople related.

There are plants and bugs and wildlife to study and catalog, and who knows what else might be out there in the pacific northwest woods. Probably not vampires or shape shifting wolves. Maybe the infamous sasquatch?

After I've had enough lying about, I venture out on foot to get acquainted with the town and to find the nearest convenience store. I grab a few essentials and something to eat from this burger place on the way back to my apartment.

Thank Mothman my furniture arrives shortly after and I have a bed to sleep on. Tomorrow, I'll venture to Port Angeles for a car, and not get fucking lost, and the day after, I start my job at the Forks Forestry Department.

I have to take a bus to Port Angeles, and then find a car dealership with a decent, reasonably priced car, which is a whole lot of peopleing for an introvert like myself. It's one of the reasons I liked the idea of moving to such a small and quiet place, even if it's a bit of a tourist attraction now. I'm glad when I'm finally finished and end up with a little yellow Beetle to drive home. I hadn't expected them to have it, and I've always wanted one.

Back at home, there's not a lot to do, which I'm perfectly fine with. My net won't be installed until a couple days from now so I pull up a playlist of Editors songs on my phone and read a book on my Kindle while I eat supper. For the rest of the evening I just bask in the Pacific northwest feels and ennui and boredom.

Tomorrow, I get to go to work.

Chapter Two

Forest

As I'm getting ready in the morning, my phone buzzes with a text.

Malcolm S: good luck Mr. Forest Ranger. You'll let me know if you find the sasquatch or some werewolves, right? And send pics!!

Malcolm is a nosey conspiracy theorist from the Ohio area who likes to search the West Virginia woods for cryptids. We met in his search for Mothman, and now, we like to yank each other's chains. He's one of those people who's always trying to get pictures of that shit. Currently he's looking for signs of the existence of the Flatwoods monster.

I think he's full of shit. I mean, I know Mothman is real, from firsthand experience but the Flatwoods monster? Come on.

Me: ty. I'll get right on that

Malcolm S: I mean it!

Me: yeah yeah

I send him a random gif of Bella in her red truck and stuff my phone in my jeans pocket. Stepping back into the bathroom, I wash my hands thoroughly so I can apply my testosterone cream. While it dries I make some coffee, toast with protein peanut butter, and slice an apple. I scarf my breakfast without really tasting it, my stomach fluttering like a swarm of moths with first day of a new job jitters.

With a heavy sigh, I pull my flannel shirt over my undershirt and head out the door. It could be worse. Starting a new job isn't nearly as stressful as say, moving and going to a new school. There's a lot less people to meet, and therefore, less people to pretend you like.

The way to work is dull, the weather is as gloomy as I imagined it'd be, and it's all so dully perfect. I park at the forestry office and give my cheeks a pat and give myself a pep talk.

"I got this. I can do this," I say feebly to my reflection in the rearview mirror as I smooth my short black curls down and push up my glasses on the bridge of my nose. No one is going to bite me. There are no vampires or werewolves in Forks. Probably.

Okay, that's enough talking to my reflection. Time for work.

When I walk into the small office, the only person in the room jolts and rises up quickly to rush over and meet me. He looks older than me, perhaps in his forties, with a hint of gray starting to blossom on the temples of his dark, mussed hair, straighter than my own. An awkward looking smile crosses his pale face, and his kind blue eyes meet my own before traveling down.

Perhaps he's assessing my plaid flannel, or the pins on each corner of my collar—one trans pride flag, one he/him pin. If it bothers him, though, his face betrays nothing. If it did, I wouldn't fucking care. I'll bite bigots.

He only smiles, though, and shoves out his hand. "I'm Jim, he/him," he says, my heart swelling at the inclusion of his pronouns. Not a bigot. Good. We'll probably get along. "You must be the new guy. Callith, was it?" He says it wrong, like cay-lith instead of cal-lith. And that's why I prefer my nickname.

"Just Cal is good," I correct him with a polite smile and shake his hand, bigger than mine and calloused.

"All right, Cal." He smiles. "Lemme show you around." He waves me forward and shoots another lopsided smile at me. "Guess there's not too much to see here, but that just makes my job easier."

The forestry department has three old and slightly worn wooden desks, one which belongs to Jim and has a couple stacks of papers, an outdated computer, and a coffee mug which says 'I [tree symbol] Forks' on it. His chair is a midback task chair in burgundy with a couple places starting to rip. Of the other two desks, one is completely blank, and the other has a matching old computer, a fresh white binder, and a metal cup with an assortment of pencils and pens in it. The task chair pushed up to this desk is pine green and less worn.

"This'll be your desk, whenever you do need it. You'll mostly be our field worker, though, as discussed in your interviews. I take care of entering your field reports into the computer and file 'em away in the cabinets back there." He points to three filing cabinets on the back wall, none of them the same color. "And there's a coffee machine and water dispenser over there."

He gestures behind me, and I glance to the opposite wall, where a small folding table is set up with a Mr. Coffee. Beside the table is a small kitchenette with a sink and a hot and cold water dispenser next to it. On the other side of the counter are a mini fridge and a microwave. All the basic necessities of a small office. Even if some of them are practically dinosaurs.

Being where I am, this doesn't surprise me one bit. On the contrary, I find it quite quaint. This is what I want. Quaint, quiet, gloomy. Perfectly dull Pacific Northwest atmosphere. Honestly? I love it. It's great.

"Cool," I say.

"I know it's nothin' special. We're still a very small town, even after... you know." He waves his hand, as if to indicate what he isn't saying, what he doesn't have to say. Even after Twilight. And he's right. The population has only grown like, one-hundred and something in the last fifteen years?

"I like it."

He smiles warmly at my reassurance. "Good, I'm glad." Jim goes to his desk and pulls open the lower drawer, grabbing out something bright orange with strips of reflector tape on it. "Here's your work vest. You'll need to wear that any time you're patrolling the forest areas, for safety reasons, you know."

"Of course." I take the vest and drape it over one arm for now.

"It'll be nice to have a fresh set of eyes out there. People who've been here all their lives get bored, you know. Who knows what you might find out there?"

Who knows, indeed. Probably not a sasquatch. But maybe. That certainly wouldn't be quiet and quaint. It wouldn't be unwelcome, though. After all, it's part of the reason I came somewhere like this. Curiosity. Research. Science. All that jazz. It'll probably turn out to be completely unremarkable, though. That's how these things go. Expect great surprises and you'll get unremarkable dullness.

Jim pulls out an actual paper map—I had no idea people even used such things anymore—and shows me all the spots circled on it. The camp grounds, the hiking trails, each of the forests. He warns me about a couple areas which might have bears or wolves as indicated on the map—just plain ol' wolves, he assures me with a wink—and hands it to me after folding it back up.

"That belonged to the previous person. It's yours now. Don't go losin' it either."

"No worries. I'll take a pic of it and pin all these in my maps app."

"See, lookit you. Already innovating. That's what this place needs, some new blood." Jim grins.

"What happened to the last person, anyways?"

Jim shrugs. "Moved on. You know how it goes sometimes." He pats my shoulder. "Well, get out there and acquaint yourself, and be careful, kid," he calls me, even though I'm not *that* young. I'm in my twenties. He seems to mean well, though, so I won't hold it against him.

"Thanks."

I take the binder and a couple pens from my desk and head back out to my Beetle. Pinning all the places on the map is a slightly tedious affair, but getting it out of the way is best. Stuffing the binder and pens in my bag, I program a route to each of the places pinned to get my bearings. Though I should introduce myself to the camp grounds managers, at some point, that's a lot of people time I'd rather not endure my first day on the job. So, I only drive by and take in the locations.

The last location on my list is one of the forest trails. Getting out there in the actual wilderness is the moment I've been waiting for. Fuck yes.

I pull on the orange vest and my backpack. It's gloomy, overcast, but not raining at the moment. I have a poncho in my backpack in the event of rain, though. One thing about being in forestry you learn quickly is to always be prepared.

Once I'm on the trail, I'm surrounded by green, green, green, and it's heaven. The trees here are old things, ancient beings, some hundreds of feet tall. The trees back in Ohio are all boring maples, and of course, buckeyes. Here, it's evergreen all around, cedars and redwoods, firs and hemlocks. When winter comes, the trees won't turn to leafless skeletons. It'll be a winter wonderland of Christmas trees, and I can't wait.

The ground is rich and springy with moisture, and there's moss covering the bases of the tree trunks and old fallen trees. Tiny hemlocks attach themselves as minions to larger trees, and sprouts of hemlock mistletoe broom outward from the branches of others. Despite being parasites, the mistletoes are best left alone. They're part of the natural ecosystem of the forest. Instead, I merely make note of them in my binder, along with the approximate location, just in case they become too invasive and turn into an infestation.

Robins chitter and woodpeckers trill in the canopy above, while bugs flit about or crawl on the ground and trunks. I jot down notes on the bark and fir dwelling beetles, assessing the condition of the trees they infest, whether there's any damage on the trunks or dead spots in the branches. For the most part it's best to leave the beetles alone as well, so long as there's less than five trees affected in an acre. Any more and I might have to request some dead trees get salvaged.

I have so many notes already. I think I might be in love.

There's a snap of a branch, and I dart my gaze around to find a deer staring right at me. When it notices me, it stares with its deep doe eyes for a moment before bounding off.

I keep heading forward.

The wildlife goes quiet. Not a thing is stirring. The hairs on the back of my neck stand on end.

Why is this place freaky all of a sudden? Why is it so quiet?

Hsssh. Hsssh. Hsssh.

At first, the sound is small, almost imperceptible. Being the only sound, though, it stands out. It sounds like... I'm not sure. It's on the tip of my tongue, but I can't quite place the sound. Whatever it is, it awakens my inner instinct to run, run, run.

I turn around and run all the way back to my car without one glance over my shoulder. Today is just getting acquainted anyways, so it's not like I needed to spend an extended amount of time here. I can come back another day, and hopefully whatever had my hairs on end will be gone.

I can't shake that strange sensation, though. My hands are shaking the whole way back to the office. Normally I don't get freaked out so easily. This is ridiculous, I know. Something about that sound set off every instinctive nerve in my body and put my hairs on end. It felt like... Like I was prey. Like I was being hunted.

When I get back to the office, Jim is leaning back in his worn chair with his Forks coffee cup in hand. Luckily, he doesn't know me well enough yet to find my behavior odd.

"How'd it go, Cal?"

"All right."

I make my way to my desk and flop into my chair. I put the map in my drawer for safe keeping and pull out the binder to log my stops for the day. When I finish—leaving out my random freaky incident of course—I pull the paper out of the rings and hand it to Jim.

He sets his coffee cup down and takes it from me, glancing over it. The writing is a little shaky, but he doesn't say anything about it. Which is good because I don't fucking care right now.

"All right, good job today, kid. If you want you can head on home."

I'm glad for the excuse. My spine is still tingling with the uncomfortable sensation of being watched. What's wrong with me?

I need a light.

Not a cigarette, I don't touch that shit. I need a literal light. Traveling across the country required packing sparsely, and that meant leaving a lot of things behind with Jezz, including my color changing LED light.

Mothman, I hope they have something at the dinky convenience store.

I end up with a LED camping lantern, which is just so perfectly Forks that I'm actually amused by it. After dropping by the burger place again for a huge bag of fries, because I'm in no mood to do the adult thing and actually buy food to cook, I set up the camping lantern in the middle of my apartment and go full blob mode on the floor, munching on my fries and getting lost in the LED glow of the lamp.

LED lets off no warmth, and is nothing compared to a real life flame, as deadly as fire is. The one upside—I won't get too hot if I glom onto this thing. The downside—I'm cold and I keep shivering. I finally move enough to yank my purple blanket from my loveseat and become a burrito.

That sound... I know that sound I heard, but I can't quite place it. All I know is it was the most chilling thing I've ever heard, like death whispering on the wind as he comes for me.

Hssssh. Hssssh. Hssssh.

I don't sleep.

Chapter Three

Web

L et's get one thing straight: I'm *not* a fucking coward, okay? I'm just *slightly* still creeped out by that neck of the woods.

That's why I do everything imaginable thing under the sun instead of go to that particular forest. Okay?

I go to all the campgrounds to introduce myself, I survey every trail except that one until there's nothing else left. This is how I pass a week.

Jezz texts me too much, asking her usual prodding questions, to which I only give brief answers, enough for her to start asking if I'm okay. Malcolm hassles me about the sasquatch a couple times and I tell him to shut up and that makes him go quiet on me.

Now I've crossed off everything else on my list and pissed off my only friends, which just leaves Jim for company, but let's face it, he's boring as all out. I have to go back to that trail and do my job, even if all my nerves are screaming at me not to.

All right. Trail. Forest. Survey. I can do this. I can do my job, and I'm not afraid of a little hssssh sound, even if it was the creepiest fucking thing I've ever heard.

It's overcast again today, the canopy of green above giving the illusion of twilight despite being before noon. The air is thick with moisture, the forest alive with sound, a good sign. For now.

I make my way along the trail, stopping to take my observations on the plants and wildlife every so often. But I never go more than a couple steps off the trail; I'm too l terrified to if I'm being honest. This particular forest trail creeps me out.

As I proceed, I'm hyper aware of every little sound, even my own feet crunching over twigs. For this reason, I'm aware as soon as the sounds die off. Only a few more steps along the path and I'm contemplating turning back for the day.

I almost run into it, looking everywhere but ahead, before a silky string catches my gaze.

It isn't a string, and it isn't just one.

It's a whole arrangement of slick, shiny strands, perfectly arranged, precisely placed in an asymmetrical circular shape.

It's a spider web.

Not a tiny one like a fly might be caught up in. It's blocking the whole pathway, and it's large enough to ensnare a deer, or even a person...

Hsssssh.

That sound is all it takes for me to turn wing and run like a bat out of hell. It's a struggle to even stay on my feet and not trip over every uneven patch of land.

My body loses control as the sound continues, as if spurring the transformation on. My on end hairs multiply into a soft, thin, velvety coat of fuzz. My antennae sprout. And lastly, my wings, the proud red-orange and yellow with two large black dots like eyes. I'm most pleased of how my moth wings have changed from the dull brown of a female io moth to the coloring of the male io since I started transitioning. In this moment, though, I'm not too proud of how I've lost control of my transformation.

Right now, I just want to get the hell out of here. I have a sinking feeling whatever is making me shift into my moth form and nearly piss myself doesn't mean well.

Hsssh. Hsssh. Hsssh. That chilling sound continues, and joining it a shifting sandpaper-like sound as whatever it is pursues me.

"*Hssssh*. You smell...deliciouss...you smell...like something to *eat*," comes a soft, raspy voice, each word carrying that distinctive *hssssh* within it somehow.

And finally, I've figured out what that sound is.

Along came a spider.

I'm not staying for dinner, though. I'm out of here. I keep running, I do not collect two-hundred dollars, I do not pass go. I'm going, going, gone.

Chapter Four

Lies

After I finally calm myself down enough to shift back to human form, I head to the office.

"Whatcha doin' back, Cal?" Jim leans forward in his chair, looking at me curiously.

"I wanted to check something on the map."

I go to my desk and pull out the thing, unfolding it on my desk. Now, where's the creepy AF forest. Ah, here it is.

There's some writing here...

Bear activity in this area.

Bears?

Yeah... My dude, they're *not* bears. They're not wolves, either. They're... Spiders. Really big spiders.

What did these spiders—spider?—look like that the previous person thought they were *bears*?! An image of a giant, hairy tarantula pops into my head. Were the *eight legs* and fangs not a giveaway? Maybe they hadn't stuck around long enough to find out. And even then, nobody would've believed a warning that said *GIANT SPIDERS* anyways. So, maybe they put bears instead, thinking a regular person would heed a seemingly normal and logical warning like bears.

And maybe, this was why the previous person had quit? And lied about what was really on that trail.

I should probably do something about this. What, though? This brings me back around to my predecessor's conundrum. I can't tell the truth. That would go over really badly. Jim would probably look at me like I have eight eyes.

The trail had been overgrown, unused in who knows how long, but maybe I should put up a sign. Jim might know something more of use, too.

"Uh, hey, Jim?" I glance his way.

"Yeah?"

"What can you tell me about this trail here?" I hold up the map to indicate where I mean.

"Oh, that one? I don't think it's used much because of the bears taking residence around there, but Spy still kept tabs on it like a champ."

"Spy...Is that who did this job before me?"

"Yeah. Spylar was his name. They were pretty meticulous, especially with that map."

"Why did they quit, then?" They obviously had a handle on things. I fully expect this Spylar lied about the bears, and knew the truth.

"He kinda kept to himself. I'm not sure he had any friends or even was too familiar with anyone in town. Guess you could call them an outcast. All Spy told me was they were moving."

"That's it?"

"Yep. Guessing he was just tired of the job or something." Jim shrugs. "Why'd you ask?"

"I was just curious is all."

"It's strange, though. Grizzly bears aren't found in the Olympic Peninsula. Usually they're up around the Cascades in the northeast. We have black bears around here."

"Huh. That is odd. Maybe they were mistaken?" Add another weird thing Meyer didn't research about Twilight to the list, too. Vampires *are* fast, so maybe Emmett did run off to the other side of Washington when he got a hankering for grizzly?

Jim shrugs. "Didn't seem like them, but it must've been a mistake."

I guess it's best not to stir the pot too much, or else I'll terrify poor Jim. Staying oblivious is probably best for him. He's too nice to drag into this.

When I get home, I do a little Googling for giant spiders. Whatever spider made a web that large and thick must be at least human sized...and it had spoken. Google is completely unhelpful, providing results for the largest known spiders in the world, which mostly reside in Brazil. I found a list of the largest spiders in the US, the largest being around six inches. That's nowhere near as large as a bear... The remaining results are horror movies. There's also a very helpful furniture ad which says "Shop for the best giant spider. Free shipping on everything, even the big stuff."

Yeah no, that's unhelpful.

I'd uncovered absolutely nothing about the cryptid I might be dealing with. A search for Pacific Northwest cryptids yields a startling amount of lake monsters, and of course the Sasquatch.

I dial Malcolm.

"What's up, Mothman? How's the job? How you likin' the rain?"

"It's okay... I did find something weird, though."

"Oh? Already? Damn, do tell!"

"Have you ever heard of giant sentient spiders?"

Malcolm laughs for a second before cutting himself off. "I'm sorry, what? Of all the things you could find out there, you think *that's* what you found? Not a Sasquatch?"

"Yeah no, it's not a Sasquatch. Has anyone ever reported the Sasquatch making enormous spider webs?"

"Guess not. You would find something entirely different than we expected. So, what're you gonna do? Spiders and moths are like, natural enemies, aren't they?"

I remember those soft, wispy words. *You smell...deliciouss...you smell...like something to eat.*

"Yeah. I guess I'm gonna do what the last guy did... Tell everyone else it's a bear and stay the hell away. I'm gonna put up a sign and close off the trail tomorrow."

"Damn. You're not going to snoop on the giant spider anymore?"

"Do you *want* me to get eaten?" I say, growling.

"Guess not. Then I'd have no scoop. At least try to get one picture for me."

"Fuck off, Mal."

He's laughing as I hang up. He knows I mean it in the most affectionate way.

The next day I get a sign board and some rope from the supply closet to do the sensible, safe thing like the boy scout I am. Or try to be.

Jim doesn't question me when I tell him I plan to close the trail due to the bear activity being so bad.

"It's gotta be black bears. Hunter's'll probably whittle 'em down during hunting season," is his only remark.

Have mercy on the hunter, I don't say aloud.

I get to the trail and hammer the sign at the entrance. It reads:

DANGER

BEARS

That should be good enough, right? I'll rope it off just to be certain.

I grab the rope out of my backpack.

"Hello," a soft voice, almost a hiss, says.

The rope falls from my hand, a gasp escaping me. What the fuck? Looking around, my eyes settle on a figure standing a few feet beyond the sign who definitely hadn't been there a second ago.

"What're you doing? Get over here." I point behind me. "This trail's dangerous. I'm closing it off to the public."

"Oh," the person says, and obeys my order, walking to my side and turning around to read the sign. "Bears?"

"Yeah." I pick up my rope again, then look at the wayward hiker.

My whole body tenses. The gaze of topaz eyes pierce through my soul, arresting me, anchoring me where I stand. Is that how Bella felt the first time she looked at Edward? I don't know. It's an odd sensation, like I've just been trapped in a snare. Like I'm the bear. And I'm about to die. Because whatever this person is, they're dangerous. More dangerous than a grizzly bear.

Words have all abandoned me. My mouth opens and nothing but a croak comes out. The hiker's skin is an unusual shade of taupe, like volcanic ash. Uneven locs frame the face of angular cheekbones and lidded eyes with upward points. It's like I'm staring down a jaguar about to pounce on me and devour me. I'm not sure whether it's fear or just plain, stunned surprise stilling me. All I do know is the hiker is the most stunningly beautiful person I've ever seen. Inhuman and achingly so, like a statue carved of onyx by the most renowned artist.

The hiker's clothing is a stark contrast to their regal features. They wear a worn plaid shirt of purple and green, and dirty black jeans with combat boots. Their frame is graceful, yet broader and more muscular than my short and slightly flabby body. Testosterone wasn't kind enough to give me a six pack. Yet. I bet this hiker has one.

"Where did they come from?" The hiker asks in that hissy, whispy voice, like a lover's caress on the ear. Like a predator's low rumble before leaping. Goosebumps bloom on my skin even though they're nowhere near my own ear.

"Huh?" I didn't comprehend the words.

"The bears."

"Oh. Um." I tear my gaze away from the snare of those eyes so I can actually fucking speak. "Dunno. Nature's unpredictable like that."

"Huh. Guess it is."

I tie the rope around the post and start stringing it towards the right tree flanking the trail entrance. "Where'd you even come from? I didn't hear you walk up. You scared the shit out of me."

"My apologies. I'm pretty light-footed." The hiker helps me loop the rope around the tree trunk, fingers brushing my own. For some reason, I get the creepy crawlies at their touch.

I shake off the odd feeling of their fingers, which were too prickly, and tie off the rope.

"Thanks. It's okay, just... Well, guess you're actually pretty safe out there if you're that stealthy. I was going to say be careful, but maybe don't sneak up on people is more appropriate?"

"I'll try not to."

I do the other rope to the left more quickly, so the strange hiker doesn't have the chance to help and possibly graze hands with me again. Except they're right behind me when I turn around, and I immediately jerk backwards, alarms sounding in my head as I bonk it on the tree.

"Ow! Fuck!"

The hiker is standing right in front of me, peering down at me with a mix of shock and concern, hands out on either side of me but not touching my shoulders. Their aroma fills my nostrils, a mix of pine, wet moss, and...and something else I can't place. Whatever it is rumbles my gut and stirs my entire body, a hunger that's core deep. My eyes dilate, the red of my inner moth trying to take over. *No!* I fight it back. I can't transform in front of a complete stranger.

"Sorry."

The hiker says words, but I'm incapable of replying again, trapped again. It's like I'm caught in the web of those eyes, waiting to be devoured, sucked dry. And yet...the thought of that is somehow thrilling rather than terrifying. They just smell so good, I can't think of anything else.

"You should go," they say. Their gaze doesn't match. It's pained now.

I'm too thankful for some distance between us. This person is so intense I can't breathe.

"Yeah," I say.

That deep hunger pain grabs my insides at the thought. It's aching, fucking agonizing. The simultaneous desires to flee and stay pin me to where I stand. If I take a single step, I'm afraid my knees will give out, and I'll tumble, and maybe the hiker will try to catch me in the clutches of their arms, too much like a trap. And then I won't be able to escape.

The hiker turns away, as if they're going to bound back onto the trail. Huh. They don't have any backpack. No gear?

"Wait!"

They look back. "Yes?"

I want to ask about the lack of gear. Going back into the woods like that is suicide. I want to tell the hiker to go home. I just closed off this trail. They can't go back on it.

"What's your name?" Is what comes out first.

"Oh. My name is Spylar Itamin. I didn't get a chance to introduce myself before."

Spylar jumps my rope with effortless grace and breaks into a run.

Spylar. Spylar. *That's* Spylar?!

"Wait! Why'd you lie about the bears?!" I shout out the first question that comes into the darkness of the mossy wilderness. No reply comes. Spylar is long gone.

Chapter Five

Along Came A Spider

I don't even know what else to say, how to articulate everything in my brain into words right now that would explain anything I just witnessed.

The thought crosses my mind that I should ask Jim more about Spylar. I'm not sure what I'd even ask.

Hey, Jim, does Spylar live in the woods?

Yeah, that'd go over real great.

So instead of doing that, I get another big bag of fries and lie on my floor, staring up at my ceiling. It's there I come to a conclusion.

Spylar lied about the bears because... They are the bears. And the bears aren't bears. They're a giant spider.

Is he like, a werespider, or something?

Why did he quit his job to live in the woods? Not that that isn't a whole ass fucking mood. I mean, life goals. Blare Hozier and run away into the woods, am I right?

I suspect I won't get a better explanation from Jim. The only way I can get answers... Is from Spylar the were(?)spider himself.

As I start to drift off, those topaz eyes fill my mind, and it's like Eyes on Fire is playing. Then there's that aroma Spylar put off... Not the wet woods, or the tree scent, but the implacable, intoxicating one, like a drug to me.

Like my own personal brand of heroin, as Edward would say.

The only choice I have which won't make me look like a weirdo is to confront Spylar for my answers. This is fine. I want to confront him. Even if part of him wants to (maybe) eat me.

Okay. I *don't* want to confront him. But I want answers. If he really is some sort of spiderperson, then we're natural enemies. I should run far, far away. I should run away screaming. This is ridiculous, and I have horrible luck. Worse than Bella.

I can see it going much like this:

"I know what you are," I would say, in the dankness of the mossy wilderness.

"Say it," Spylar might say, if they've seen the movie.

"Werespider." I would gulp before saying the word aloud.

"What do I eat?"

"Moths."

Yeah, right. That's not gonna happen. There I go fantasizing about Twilight again. It's funny, in an ironic way. I read the books shortly out of high school, and I mean, I liked them *okay*, but I wasn't a Twihard by any means. I didn't get all attached or emotional over it or anything.

After I started transitioning, though, for some reason, I started getting into it again. I rewatched the movies and reread the books. Maybe it was when *Midnight Sun* was released, and all the Twilight hype started coming on hard again, the Twilight renaissance, or resurgence, or whatever you wanna call it. Getting to read Edward's side, now being a trans guy, just clicked for me somehow.

I also got way more outdoorsy, suddenly enjoying hiking and camping and shit. I'd pack up a bunch of protein bars and go exploring hiking trails. The Pacific Northwest had been calling my name for awhile before I moved.

Now that I'm here, the last thing I expected was to meet my own impossible ill-fated supernatural being. Yeah, part of me wants to confront him. Another part, louder and screaming, wants me to run away.

They could kill you. They said you smelled delicious, for fuck's sake, Cal!

Get it together, Cal....

But those eyes...

But those *fangs*...

I give myself a few days to forget the look of them and the smell of him and those damn eyes on fire. My conscious mind does a so-so job. My unconscious mind dreams about him.

My mornings and evenings are spent jogging to wear myself out, ignoring prying texts from Jezz and Mal, and scarfing a burger and fries or a protein bar.

I make a trip over to La Push, for the hell of it. La Push, baby. There's no guy there to flirt with and coax into telling me a scary and enlightening story.

The last guy in my life had been Sunil, who everyone thought was good for me except for the one person who mattered: me. My mom said I would learn to love him. Yet Sunil wouldn't learn to love me.

He wanted me to change for him. He wanted me to match this perfect image of an old fashioned wife for him, who cooked and gave him a pack of kids. Sunil wanted me to be traditional. He wanted me to be pretty and clean shaven from underarms to toes.

He wanted me to be a woman. But I'm not.

It took a couple years but I was so excited when my beard started coming in. Now I have a full face of dark hair. There's some on my chest and legs, too, thicker than it used to be.

I shove Sunil out of my mind. He's part of the reason I wanted to get away and start over.

A beach jog doesn't clear my mind. The only thing that will, I guess, is to get it the hell over with and talk to Spylar.

I mentally prepare myself for my imminent interaction with Spylar.

I will not let those eyes on fire bewitch me, I won't let that smell they put off invite me in, and I refuse to be afraid.

Despite my inner pep talk, I'm shaking when I enter the trail. Fear clamps at my spine, fluttering in my belly like moth's wings.

Birds and other small creatures chitter and chatter as I go past my barricade and deeper in. Nothing's amiss so far. No weird *hssssh*. No tinglies at my neck. No webs. No Spylar.

So, I keep going deeper into the woods.

"Spylar? Are you here?"

A bird squawks and flies off somewhere nearby. I jump out of my skin. Fucking birds.

"Spylar?"

Taking a few more steps, I keep scanning the area. The crunch of leaves and a low rumble hits my ears. I dart my gaze in that direction.

A behemoth of a black bear creeps towards me. I freeze where I am.

"Get out of here, bear!" I say in a loud voice, attempting to scare it while putting my arms out and waving them. "You don't want anything to do with me."

The bear remains fixated on me.

"I don't have anything you want. I'm not trying to get in your space. Move along now. Okay, buddy?" I continue the movement of my arms, like I'm fluttering my wings. "Go on!"

Screeeeech, a bird sounds out of nowhere.

"Ahh!!" I echo, a knee jerk reaction. Hopefully the bear is as scared by the sound as I am.

The bear growls. My whole body tenses.

It turns away and runs off, and I let out a heavy breath I didn't know I was holding.

The ground crunches behind me, and I whirl, too fast, losing my balance and falling backward.

"Ah!"

"Are you okay?" A familiar, whispy voice says.

Spylar looks down at me with those penetrating topaz eyes, laced with more concern than should be appropriate for someone I barely know. He offers his hand, and I take it without thinking. A shiver shoots through me, my fingers tingling as if touched by a thousand prickly hairs, as if he's Peter Parker or something, which I guess, he sort of is?

I pull my hand from their grasp as soon as I'm on my own two feet. He's dressed in all black today, almost imperceptible except for his topaz eyes, twin flames in the darkness of the heavy canopy overhead. Without any daylight creeping through, he'd be the night itself.

"What are you doing out here?" He asks, head turning, locs falling over his shoulder in a way I can only describe as endearing. An endearing predator. Seemingly nice...until they have me right where they want me to move in for the kill.

"You live in the woods?" I ask, even though I'm absolutely certain I know the answer.

"I do."

"You used to work at the forestry department." That one isn't a question. I'm definitely absolutely certain this is true. Spylar is a strange name, especially for a small town.

"I did." He sticks his hands in his pockets. Plotting? Or relaxing?

"I think I know what you are." I think. I'm not absolutely positive.

"Will you tell me what you are if I tell you the truth?" he counters.

I wince. Did he see my wings that day?

"Fine." It seems like a fair trade at this point. No one would believe either of us anyways.

"So, what do you think I am?" He steps closer. I resist the urge to step back. They smell so fucking good, it's hard to concentrate.

"Like a...a werespider?" I say after an embarrassing pause.

Spylar chuckles, a bright sound which lightens my chest in a not unpleasant way. Their breath wisps against my lips, and it's like I'm inhaling a drug. Like this scent was made specifically for me and me alone, to reel me in, drawn like the helpless moth I am to a flame.

"Just a spiderperson."

A spiderperson. Okay. Fine. This is fine.

It's not fine. It's terrifying.

"Now you," he prompts after a moment of silence. "What's your name?"

"I. I'm... Cal Morri. And I'm... a mothman. We call ourselves mothpeople, or mothmx." Somehow, I manage a step back. I still can't breathe without smelling him. It's like being buzzed.

He steps closer again, and speaks into my ear. I wonder if the chill he gives me is a thrill for him, being on the prey's side of this "Then you understand why it's a horrible idea for you to be here. Alone. With me. You should be running, while you still can." His words are like silk thread, spinning through my ears, pleasant and unpleasant all at once.

He's right. I should run. We're natural enemies.

There is a part of me that wants to do exactly that. But the other part of me is strangely thrilled instead of chilled.

"My sense of self preservation must be broken. It's probably too late to exchange it for another one."

He laughs, light and in that whispy way of his, yet still somehow loud. "It must be. Why were you looking for me?"

"I..." My face is hot. I hate how much he flusters me; it makes me feel like I'm in high school. "I couldn't stop thinking about you. I had to know what you really were, and why you just... left and went off the grid."

I'm thankful they've put more distance between us, and it's easier to think that way. He moves towards a tree and leans against the trunk. "I've always had trouble being around people. Trouble blending in. Truth is, I got tired of forcing myself to live a human existence. It was exhausting." His head falls back against the tree, eyes closing. Relaxed. Not ready to pounce. There is no doubt in my mind they could easily change gears, faster than I could react, from laid back to cold killer.

"So, you made up the bear thing... and chose one of the abandoned trails, so people would leave you alone?"

His head nods infinitesimally. "That's about the gist of it."

"What about your family? Do you have any, found or blood?"

"I don't speak to them much. Spiders are very solitary creatures. We have a tendency to go our separate ways as we age."

"Oh. I'm sorry."

Their eyes open. "Why?"

"Well, um... aren't you lonely?"

Spylar shrugs. "It is what it is."

Part of me thought he'd say no. It had been a redundant question on my part. He said spiders were solitary. Probably patient, too, having to wait for their food to come to them.... I shiver and push away that thought.

"So... If I came again, would you want the company?"

Their eyebrows rise. "You trust me enough to be alone in the woods with me?"

"You've had plenty of chances to do me in already and you haven't yet."

His face turns grimmer than a reaper. "I'm not sure what the limits of my control are. I could still end up hurting you."

"I know you can control yourself. You've not lost control yet." I move closer to him of my own volition, putting myself willingly in danger, in the heat of the irresistible flame that is Spylar Itamin, my natural enemy, my inevitable yet sweet demise.

Spylar inhales my scent slowly, like a fine incense. "It is a little lonely out here." He smiles.

"I'm trusting you not to let your instincts win. Don't let me down, okay?"

Spylar nods, reaching a hand up to touch my face, stroking prickly fingers feather light over my skin. My beard blocks some of the prickliness, until their fingers continue downwards along my neck. I shudder and gasp, getting a fuller breath of his heady scent. My skin tingles all over, my inner moth fluttering anxiously to come out, to be closer to the one who is like flame and fear, desire and disaster. Of all the myths and legends I could have encountered, along came a spider.

"A moth," he says.

"A spider." I make myself step back, a task equal parts painful and prudent.

And so the lion fell in love with the lamb... Or, more accurately, the moth fell in love with the spider.

"So, what brought you to this town, anyways?" They ask.

"Work... Sort of. And a weird and unhealthy Twilight fixation." My face heats at admitting the last part aloud.

"What's that?" He looks confused.

"What?" I have no clue what part of what I said is confusing.

"Twilight."

"Wait... You're telling me you live in fucking *Forks* and you don't know about Twilight?!"

"I kept to myself most of my life, so I can't say I'm very with the times." He shrugged, as if missing a pop culture phenomenon that's still shaping the landscape of media today is no big deal at all.

"Okay, wow. I'll bring you a copy of the first book next time I visit, then."

"So, you actually want to see me again?" He smiles, a little shyly, a little hopefully, and reaches one hand out, caressing my cheek with the back of their hand this time, which is much softer. Had he noticed, I wonder, how I shuddered at the feel of his fingers?

"Yeah. My sense of self preservation is fucked up, remember?"

Their smile widens. "Right. Next time, then?" Spylar strokes my cheek one more time before pulling their hand away.

"Same Bat time, same Bat place."

"What?"

"Batman?" He still looks confused. "Okay. Adding that to the list."

Spylar's head tilts to one side. "There's a list now?"

"Yup, I guess so."

No big deal. Just making a bucket list with a spider. Things to do before we die or they kill me.

"Okay." He smiles. A charming smile. A devious smile. Most certainly a smile which'll be the death of me. Whether that's literally or figuratively yet, I'm not sure. "I look forward to it."

"Right. Uh." I forget myself for a moment again. "See you tomorrow."

"See you tomorrow, Cal. I'll be the one on the spider web." Their whispy, silken voice trails me, lingering in my head long after I leave, stuck to me like webs.

I'm already well and truly caught up in Spylar's web. Along came a spider indeed.

Chapter Six

Scary Stories

B less fucking Hot Topic in the queer of our lord. I've been looking for a use for the Twilight journal and pen I bought there, and Spylar and Cal's Bucket List is as good as any.

Item one: Spylar needs to read the Twilight books.

Item two: watch Twilight movies together.

Item three: Batman (the 60s show)

Item four: The Batman (with Robert Pattinson, ironically)

We'll add more as needed, which I'm sure will happen, since Spylar isn't kidding about living under a rock (or more accurately, in the woods). I wonder if he really just... Chills, like out in the woods, hanging from his web, or if he has a cabin or hut in the middle of the woods somewhere. If they don't, what will they do in the winter? Hibernate?

For fuck's sake, they're not a bear. What do real spiders do?

I could Google it.

Oh... Apparently they do kinda hibernate. It's called diapause. And they usually seek out trees, rocks, or leaves to chill out in a kinda suspended state while winter does its thing. I wonder if Spylar will do that once it's winter...

If I survive until then. There's still a chance this could end badly. I don't know what they're capable of. And in his spider form, when or if I even see it, Spylar might be some frightening or out of control. Who knows what could happen?

Our friendship is one big scary story, unfolding before me now. The biggest horror of it all, though? I don't fucking know what to expect next. All I can do for now is acquire Spylar a copy of Twilight (easy to find in the home of Twilight, they literally have them in the gift shops), and show up at the same time, same place tomorrow.

And so I do exactly that.

During my rounds, in the early afternoon, I go to the trail where Spylar dwells. In the area around where we agreed to meet, between two trees, a gigantic web has been woven. As with a garden variety spider, it popped up overnight out of nowhere.

Near the top of the web, a mass of silk is perched in the branches like a hammock, and in it, Spylar lounges. He still looks human, no extra legs or hair sprouted, and I wonder again if he might show that side to me, or if they think it might terrify me too much. Being what I am, it wouldn't surprise me.

One thing at a time, I guess. Baby steps.

"Hello, Cal," they say, leaping down and landing swiftly and gracefully as an angel of death before my feet.

Not human. Not human at all, despite looking like one at the moment.

When I'm not in moth form, I have no special or enhanced abilities. Apparently, that's not the case with spider people.

"Uh. Hi."

They stand up tall, more than a few inches taller than me, and I'm captive to those eyes all over again, flustered all over again, fucked up all over again.

"How are you?" He asks. Spylar's not close enough for me to smell their intoxicating scent, but I'm already bracing myself for it. He's dazzling enough without that added in, with his skin like coal, his eyes like embers.

"F-Fine." I pull the backpack from my shoulders and fumble through it. "I've brought your assigned reading for our book club," I say, holding up Twilight and an Edward pen with a grin. "And a pen, in case you feel like notating it."

"Thanks." He takes them both, stuffing the pen in a pocket and looking over the book. "So, this is required reading, huh?"

"Yep. You literally live in the woods around Forks, and it takes place in Forks."

"And... It's about vampires?" Spylar asks after reading the back.

"Yep. Forks was basically a nowhere town that just happened to be in the Olympic peninsula and is, like, one of the cloudiest, rainiest places in the United States, so that's why the author chose it. It's still a nowhere town, but now it's something of a tourist spot. You really didn't know this?"

Spylar shrugs. "Can't say I paid much mind to much of anything in town."

"You really do live under a rock."

They give me a sheepish smile. "Sorry."

"Don't be sorry." I offer my own smile. "I'm here to help educate you about pop culture, now."

He chuckles. "Starting with this."

"Yep. Starting with Twilight. It's the most relevant, obviously."

"Obviously," he echoes, and stashes the book in his jacket.

"So, um... Since I know about you and all... Will you let me do a proper survey of the area?"

Spylar's head tilts to one side as as he considers my question. "Sure."

"Cool. Do you wanna walk with me while I do that?"

They nod.

We begin our walk, sticking to the trail. Spylar walks beside me, enough distance between us for his bewildering and bewitching effect not to take over my mind and senses.

A cluster of moss with bugs on it catches my interest, and I squat to do a quick inspection.

"So, what do you eat?" I can't imagine tiny bugs would satiate a human sized spider.

"Whatever makes its way into my web. Deer or rabbits mostly. The bears are too strong to get stuck in the webs. A lot of bugs get caught up, so I eat those, but it takes a lot of them to get full. Sometimes that's all I get for days and days."

"Wow." I stand up again, glancing at their face. One hundred percent serious. "You don't eat any human food?"

"I can, but it's just not the same. Having to chew feels unnatural."

I'm not sure I want to know the details of that statement. Maybe a subject change would be good...

"Do you keep a cabin in the woods somewhere?"

"I do. It's more of a treehouse." Again, Spylar speaks so earnestly, like it's no biggie he lives in the woods like an actual spider.

I wonder if I'll see his spider form at some point... Or if they think it might scare me away. I'm not sure I'm quite ready. For now, I'll remain blissfully unaware of the monstrous side of Spylar, instead enchanted by this beautiful human shaped version.

"What will you do when it gets colder? Do spider people go into diapause?"

"Yes. I practically *will* live under a rock when it gets too cold."

"Wow. I can't imagine just going off the grid like you did. I mean, good for you. So many people say they just want to run away into the woods, and here you go actually doing it."

Spylar lifts a shoulder in a half shrug. "I suppose it's easier when you've never been good at being human."

Mothmx must be better at being human. When we're not in moth form, we're indistinguishable to humans. To other moths, we put off a particular scent, which signals other moths. We tend to congregate because of this. Chances are if you know one moth in a friend group, the majority or even all of them are actually mothmx.

Maybe it works this way for spider people, too? It makes sense.... I'm drawn in by the scent of Spylar. Being natural enemies, it stands to reason this is the case. And it's not one sided, either. I still remember those first whispered words, of how delicious I smelled.

Have any other spider and moth people ever met, and realized the strange chemical reaction as we have? This combination is fierce, possibly deadly. Spylar could be resisting his spider instincts right now, thinking of how to entrap me in his webs and suck the life out of me.

And I've chosen to be their friend. I've chosen potential danger and horror. This could end badly. As in I became the fucking meal. Only this isn't some romantic young adult novel. This is real life, and real life doesn't always get happy endings where love triumphs over everything.

I want to ask Spylar more about how they feel. About if they want to eat me. But the desire to remain blissfully unaware wins out for now.

Our relationship is a horror story in the making. And I'm not big on horror. I sleep with a night light, and not just because I'm a mothman. I'm legit a tiny bit scared of the dark.

I've chosen the night over the light. I've chosen the unknown, uncertainty.

This could end badly.

This could end badly.

That's all I can think as we walk and we talk.

We circle back around to the beginning of the trail, and I'm ashamed to admit I spent most of the walk thinking of how Spylar might ruin me instead of doing my job.

"Well. This is my stop," I say, shoving my hands in my pockets and pivoting on my feet. "I have to go back to the office. But I can stop by again after I punch out, if you want?"

"I'd like that."

He's stepped closer without me noticing, like he's got super speed, which maybe he does. One coal hand reaches up, stroking my cheek with the back of their palm, the softer side again. This does nothing to calm my smoldering, magma core. My heart is so quick now I could practically be a hummingbird.

"Maybe I can ask the questions then?"

His hopeful eyes ignite a flame within me. I stare into them unabashed while my face burns as brightly as my insides. I commit those eyes to memory, sear them onto my soul, as if this could be the last time I see them. In truth, every time could be the last time. Every moment with Spylar could be my last.

I want to ask if he feels this with even one iota of the ferocity I do, but I have no words at the moment. I might as well be trapped in their web, as arresting as their smoldering gaze is.

I'm Icarus, and I'm flying too close to the sun. I'm going to get burned. Yet it's not going to stop me from coming back over and over again to test my luck.

No response other than a resounding, "Yeah," comes out of my mouth, just as I expected.

I'm already doomed, already past the point of no return, knowingly treading on thin ice. Despite this, my gut turns with excitement and anticipation.

I've made my decision. There's no other choice I could've even made, as drawn to Spylar as I am. Staying away is as futile as a moth resisting the draw of a lamplight.

And it's exactly this futile struggle which brings me back to Spylar's trail after work. There's no other choice.

My feet carry me true and swift, though I try not to outright run like a lovesick highschool student. Spylar's ember eyes shine from the tree hammock, and it sets my soul alight. They land before me, their scent so intoxicating I might faint.

No other choice. Moth to a flame. He draws me in with those eyes on fire and then he'll catch me in his web, and I'll never escape. But I don't want to.

"H-Hi," I choke out, damn my nerves.

"Hello, Cal." Their silk voice says my name like a lover's caress.

I stifle the urge to move closer. "Did you read any while I was gone?"

"A couple chapters. So, this Bella girl... Just willingly moved to Forks even though she hated it?"

"Yep. Pretty ridiculous, right?"

Spylar nods. "Just a little."

I stand at the trunk of the tree Spylar's hammock is built in, glancing up at it curiously. Questions spin like webs in my mind. It's Spylar's turn to ask the questions, though.

"Do you want to go on the hammock?" They ask. "It's not sticky like my webs, I promise."

I consider the option. The height isn't an issue. I can fly if I want to in my moth form. And I highly doubt Spylar would do something as murderous or cruel as shoving me into the nearby web, which probably is sticky. Even if they have a craving for me.

"Sure." I can't be more doomed than I already am.

Spylar offers a hand, hoisting me effortlessly into his back when I take it.

"Hold on tight, spider monkey," I say.

"What?"

"Nothing. You'll get that joke down the line."

They go up the tree like Spider-Man and let me off their back into the hammock. When Spylar lowers themself into it as well, it dips, forcing us to press against each other, side by side. My face burns and my nerves are all on fire every place we touch.

"Is this okay?"

"Um. Yeah," I say.

I mean it's... Very overstimulating. In a good way, though.

"So.... You're a mothman."

"Yep. I'm an io moth."

Spylar tilts their head. "There's different breeds?"

"Yep. Any of the different types of moths you can think of, there are probably mothmx of as well. Luna moths, rosy maples, atlas moths... And the list goes on. Is it like that for spider people?"

He touches my lips with the back of his fingers. "My turn right now, remember?"

My mind concocts an image of those lips touching mine instead of their fingers, heating up my face again. At least some of it is covered by my beard.

"What is the io moth like?"

"The io has different coloration according to sex. Males are shades of yellow or orange, with dark spots like eyes on each wing. Females are shades of brown. Which is annoying if you're trans or nonbinary. The best thing for me about transitioning has been the change in my wing color."

Spylar smiles. "I'm glad your body can match your gender, even in moth form. I'm nonbinary myself and use he or they pronouns interchangeably. I'm not very particular. Gender is mostly a hassle to me."

"That's cool. I noticed Jim at the forestry department used both for he and they for you, so I wondered. Thanks for telling me."

The free exchange of this info is bolstering. Even if I already suspected Spylar was queer, it's nice knowing they accept me. Being queer is continually coming out, always on a precipice of *will this person turn out to be a bigot?* As with coming out, the relief never stops, either. It's a huge weight off every time.

"Is your whole family moths?"

"Yeah. We're all Io moths. There's my parents and my younger sister, Jezz. She's kinda protective of me."

Spylar smiles warmly, a smile I could easily get caught up in. "It must've been hard for her, you moving here. Where is it you're from?"

"Ohio, close to the border of West Virginia. AKA mothmx country."

"Oh." He half laughs. "That's where most of the mothmx live, I guess?"

"Yeah. I'm kinda going out on my own, moving to the Pacific Northwest. Mothmx are usually very social. We even have a yearly festival just for meeting up...and hooking up."

Spylar listens intently, eyes on me like fire catching on brush. It's an intense thing. An embarrassing thing.

"Wow. I never knew there were other cryptids, and with their own customs, too."

"I never suspected there was anything like you out there, either. I always wondered if there were other cryptids, but I never dreamed of spiderperson, of all things."

Spylar's gaze turns ahead, set on nothing in particular. Rain is trickling around us, the canopy of leaves shielding us from the wetness.

"I wouldn't dream of me, either. I'm having trouble imagining why you want to be friendly with me, actually..." They turn to me again, leaning in enough for their breath to caress my skin as they continue, "Do I smell as tempting to you as you do to me?"

Yes. Fucking A, yes. I don't say it aloud like that. It's a damn good thing he can't read thoughts. Those burning eyes bore into me, melt me to my core, and his sweet breath is like honey. It's impossible to think, or remain composed. Fuck.

I'm not the only one, apparently. The idea of having some sort of effect on him the way he does me is thrilling. Moth's wings flutter in my belly.

I nod, infinitesimally. "You do."

They reach out a hand, splaying fingers and palm along my neck, thumb grazing the center of my collarbone. The strange pads of his fingers press on the flesh of my neck, spreading goosebumps.

"It should be a crime for someone to smell so mouth-watering. Why do our bodies do this to us?"

I tremble and swallow. The goosebumps spread. Fuck if I know the answer to that question. The fates are cruel. Nature is cruel. I say nothing.

"Do you think my touch is unpleasant?"

I shake my head. "It's not that. It's just... Unusual."

I don't want to say I dislike it. That's not necessarily true. I mean, it gives me goosebumps something fierce. It's also exciting, and thrilling, and it's like I'm in danger, but I don't want it to stop. I don't want to say I dislike it, because I don't want Spylar to stop.

"Do you want me to stop?" Their hand pauses, the heat of it still making my nerves all abuzz where the digits hover.

I swallow. "No."

His fingers press against my flesh again, set my soul alight again. He just strokes them gently along my neck and collar, nothing else, but fuck.

"Will you tell me more about your moth form?"

I nod infinitesimally. It's hard to concentrate with their touch.

"So... I have wings, yellow with a large pair of dots. Short yellow antennae. Red eyes. Yellow fur." I swallow between sentences. My throat burns from his soft and prickly touch.

"Would you show me sometime?"

I want to ask them the same, but it's not my turn. I wonder if the effects we have on each other will be stronger in those forms. Would his spider instincts win, and put me to an end? This would be our trial, our test.

"S-Sure."

"Are you afraid?"

"Kinda." Afraid I'll lose him. Afraid I'll lose my life. These war in my head, competing with his prickly touch.

They remove their hand, eyes pinching together. "I'm sorry."

"No. Don't be," I say, taking his hand.

Prickly fingers clasp over the back of my hand. They lift it to their face, pulling my fingers down along their cheek. Their skin is velvety here. I keep feeling when his hand drops from mine.

"I don't want you to make yourself stay if you're afraid, or think I'm repulsive."

"Fuck, Spylar... I don't think that at all. I'm not scared because I find you frightening or repulsive. I mean, sure, part of my moth instinct is screaming at your touch. But the human part of me? That part is like, fuck, they're hot."

Spylar chuckles, exposing vampire-like fangs. "Hot?"

"Sexy. Attractive. Beautiful." My fingers stroke tiny circles into the soft skin of Spylar's cheeks, while my lips long to be kissing in-between those words.

"So are you, Cal."

My face heats as my mouth tilts upward. His hand lifts to touch my cheek again, stroking my beard. For a long time, minutes or maybe longer, we stay like this. Touching, staring, longing. Nothing else.

The rain dies down and the woods are darkening.

"I guess I should go before it gets too dark."

"Okay," Spylar says, but doesn't make any attempt at moving.

I'm the first one to pull my hand back. He takes us back down to the ground, an awkward moment of silence passing between us until I say, "See you tomorrow?"

"Until then, Cal."

I stare at his smile and his eyes for an embarrassing amount of time before I finally move.

"Okay. Bye," I finally say.

This whole situation really is a scary story unfolding before me. I never imagined this is what I'd end up falling into when I moved here, not in all my wildest dreams or nightmares.

Chapter Seven

Mind Over Matter

The next day is busy, with me turning in paperwork on Spylar's trail finally, and checking up on some of the campgrounds.

When I get to Spylar at the end of my work day, they zip down from their web to meet me, sliding down on a line of web, Twilight book open in hand.

"This book is ridiculous! But I can't stop reading."

I laugh. "Yeah, I know. It has that effect. It's like, it's not particularly good, but the premise and the suspense are good enough for you to get sucked in."

"Exactly." He drops to his feet and closes the book. "Did you move here because of this book?"

My face burns. "Um. Well, partly. I also just happened upon the opportunity with the forestry department, so it kinda seemed like fate."

"Have you been drawing parallels between us, and Bella and Edward?"

Oh no. Somehow, my face burns hotter. Maybe letting them read this book was a bad idea. What had I been thinking?

"Uh. Maybe a little?" I stare at the ground.

"How much is a little?" They take my chin and tilt it up, so I have to look at them, my burning cheeks unshielded from their burning gaze.

"Do I have to answer that?"

"No. I could always make you, though."

"Pff." I force myself to step back. "You're bluffing."

He grins, showing off his fangs. "Am I? You don't know the limits of what I'm capable of."

That's true. There's still a lot to learn about Spylar, and so much I want to ask.

"Are you, then?"

Thankfully, Spylar shakes their head. "I don't have any mind tricks that I'm aware of. But..." Their lips purse. "It doesn't mean you're safe. You might be as reckless as Bella."

"Probably." I smile, despite how fucking morbid this conversation has turned. "What chapter are you on?"

"Balancing. Can we talk about how offensive this description of Billy Black is?! What the hell?" They shove the book in my face, opened to an underlined segment describing Billy. That's not the only thing he's underlined, either. He's been going to town on this book. I read over the sentences in question to jog my memory.

"Wow. Okay, yeah, what the fuck, Stephenie? I'll say that the shittiest part about Twilight is her using the Quileutes as a plot device. Edward is a tiny bit creepy, too."

"I agree, that is shitty."

"Yeah. It has its issues. I think it's important we recognize that and take our own measures to be better. I've donated to the Quileutes' fund to relocate to higher ground myself."

Spylar smiles. "That's great."

"So, what would you like to do today?"

"We could take a hike, and talk about this book. I have other notes."

I snort. "I noted that."

Spylar grins. "There's a lot I have questions about. The things that pass for popular fiction are ridiculous."

"You're not wrong."

I fall into step beside him and we follow the trail deeper into the woods, further from society. Where no one would hear me scream. In pain or pleasure is yet to be known.

"Whose turn is it for twenty questions today?" I ask.

"What do you say to a free for all? You ask your questions and I'll ask mine."

"Sure." There's so much I want to ask them, and I'm certain most of their questions today will be about their numerous notes on Twilight.

"I find Edward and Bella's conversations interesting. I can't tell whether they like each other or not. They bicker a lot."

"Yeah. She's a bit stubborn, and doesn't like that he won't tell her what he is. But also, he dazzles her, because he's, you know, a vampire."

"Right. It does make me wonder if that's all it is, though, you know? Just her being dazzled."

Just her being dazzled. Sticks and brush crunch beneath our feet, the gentle sway of a breeze rustling the canopy above us. These are the only sounds around us. The creatures of the forest avoid us. Avoid *Spylar*. Because they're a predator.

Dazzled. It's because I'm being dazzled. For as much as he scares me and makes my hairs stand on end and makes my instincts scream at me to run run run, they also are alluring.

Dazzling. But what if it's all just instinct, just a matter of chemistry?

"Cal?"

I jump out of my skin. My foot catches on something and throws me off. "Fuck!" I twist, swiveling in a horrible attempt to regain my balance. Spylar catches one of my wrists, but I'm already leaning too far.

My back hits a tree. Spylar is right there, almost nose to nose with me, his other hand on my hip. His damp, mossy scent fills my lungs. Chemistry. They are made to draw me in. It must be a spider thing. I'm part insect, after all.

The way he turns my stomach, though. Moth's wings rage in my belly. It's not mere chemistry, is it?

"Are you all right?" they ask, their breath mingling with mine.

"Y-Yeah," I choke out, struggling not to let my lips brush theirs. They damn near do.

"Cal?" His head tilts, inquisitively, doing nothing to put our lips further apart.

"Hm?"

"Do I... Dazzle you?"

I don't want to answer that fucking question. Because the answer, most certainly, is yes. I'm so fucking dazzled I can't think straight when I'm around him. Instead, I shift infinitesimally closer, tilting my head the opposite way of theirs. Our lips brush. My soul ignites. Every single hair on my body stands on end.

The brushing of lips, not even a kiss, is only for an instant before Spylar shifts away.

"Unlike fiction, I'm a real danger to you," they say, hanging their head and rubbing a hand over their scalp.

"I don't care."

Spylar glances up, but doesn't meet my eyes. "Do you not value your life?"

"You won't hurt me. You would've already."

He shakes his head, rubs his hands over his face. "I could still hurt you. I don't know."

I step forward and take his hands away so I can look into his eyes. "You won't."

"But I want to. I want to fill your body with my venom and suck the life out of you. It would be so much better if you did want to run."

"I won't. I don't know what's good for me." I smile and squeeze their hands. "Do you want the honest truth? I *am* dazzled."

"That's exactly why I'm worried. You won't be scared when you *should* be." They wrench their hands away from mine, turn away from me, and clutch their locs. "You won't know when you should *run*."

Why the fuck is he sounding like Edward all of a sudden? What did I miss? Is this all because I tripped? Maybe I shouldn't have let them read that damn book.

"Spylar... I think you're getting too into the book. It's *fiction*."

"You're right. It *is* fiction. And unlike fiction, you're in *real* danger." I grab for their hand, only for them to pull it away.

"Prove it, then." I put as much stubbornness as possible in my words of challenge. Spylar hasn't hurt me yet. They're just letting this book get in their head. He won't hurt me.

"What?"

"You heard me. Fucking prove it. Prove you would hurt me. Because you haven't yet. So, I don't believe you." I stand straight and cross my arms, giving my best authoritative look.

Spylar continues shaking and clutching their head.

"I'll come back tomorrow. Read the next chapter before then."

It's a silly notion, but maybe if Spylar reads Edward putting mind over matter, they'll have the faith to do it as well.

"What difference would that make?" He turns his head to the side, only enough to see me out of his periphery.

"Just trust me. It might help."

He sighs and nods. "Okay. See you tomorrow?"

"Yeah. Tomorrow is Saturday, so I could come in the morning, early. If you want?"

"Okay. I'll be waiting," they say, lower-voiced, expectantly, in a way which churns my stomach with a mix of fear and anticipation.

"O-Okay."

We circle back around to the trail entrance in somewhat awkward silence.

"Good night," I say, waving.

"Good night, Cal. Pleasant dreams." Their voice carries a note of melancholy which upsets me.

With any luck, tomorrow all will be made clear.

My sleep is neither peaceful or pleasant, despite Spylar's farewell wishes. A nauseating mix of fear and nervousness thrums in my belly, and by about four a.m. I give up attempts to sleep and go about my morning routine of showering, trimming my beard up a bit, and scarfing down some protein cereal. Mmm cardboard goodness.

I flip halfheartedly through my ebook of Twilight, brushing myself up in preparation for today. Will Spylar glean what I want him to from the chapter in the meadow? Images come to my mind of Spylar, more spider-like, zipping around the clearing at deadly speeds, showing me what they are capable of, how easily they could outmatch and overpower me, and in the moment, I am frightened. But I'm also resigned to my fate. I couldn't stay away from him if I tried now.

It's too late.

I wait until a somewhat decent hour of eight o' clock to head over to the trail, bringing some blankets and snacks with me in case I end up wanting to spend the whole day with Spylar. Hopefully, I won't end up being chased away. Or become the meal.

The woods are still waking up when I arrive, quiet birdsongs in the trees and morning dew on the leaves creating an ambience which calms my fluttering nerves.

Spylar is hanging from his web, upside down, book in his face.

"Hi," I say from the base of the tree.

They remove the book from in front of their eyes and slide gracefully down the string of web to land before me.

"Good morning." Spylar wears shades of brown today, a dark brown t-shirt with a light brown leather jacket over it.

I look down at my own red plaid, hopes of accidentally matching quashed. Oh well.

"How are you feeling?"

Spylar shrugs. "Good, for now. I think I know what I need to do. So ask me again after our test of faith?"

"You got it. So, where to today?"

They smirk, and it's entirely too dazzling on them. Yet again I'm floored by how dashing Spylar is.

"If this book is any indication, maybe a nice meadow would be appropriate?"

I nod. "Uh. Have any of those handy?"

"I think I know where one is."

"Well then, lead the way."

"As you wish."

Spylar moves with a swiftness I don't possess, just quick enough to leave my pathetic normal humanoid feet a few places behind him all the way to our destination. No matter how many times I try to catch up, move at a jog when the landscape permits, I never can gain on them.

It's a frustrating fucking game and I'm not amused. I'm regretting my decision to give him that book again.

Spylar disappears through a mash of bushes, and I, on my last straw, growl and sprint through after them. I slam into a strong back. Spylar doesn't budge an inch on impact.

"Fuck!"

"Sorry," they say. "We're here." They turn around and take my hands in theirs, prickly fingers raising my hairs, and lead me slowly into the clearing.

I give him a pouty glare. "Why'd you stay so far ahead of me?"

"Part of me thought you might give up on me." I squeeze his hands, frowning. "Another part of me wanted to further prove my abilities to you. Speed is just one thing I'm capable of."

"I'm not going anywhere. So stop trying to make me, for fuck's sake."

It doesn't slip my notice Spylar keeps their grip loose. Like he'll change his mind for the both of us and just disappear.

"The question is, will you still be thinking that after you see me today?"

"Why wouldn't I?" We're in the middle of the small meadow when Spylar stops and releases my hands. Sitting down in the grass, I look up at them.

One of Spylar's eyebrows raises. "Have you ever seen a spiderperson?"

"I've watched the Spider-Man movies. Does that count?"

Spylar kneels a few feet away, looking clueless about my remark. "I'm not sure what that is."

"Okayyyy, another thing for our bucket list, then. He's a superhero with spider-like abilities."

"I assure you, he's probably less terrifying than me. Superheroes look friendly, do they not?"

"Generally, yeah."

"I'm closer to a villain than a hero. I'm a monster." The way they state this so plainly, without remorse, clenches my heart.

"Just because you look like a monster, doesn't mean you're the villain."

He doesn't seem comforted by my statement. "I would reserve your judgment until you see."

I offer only a noncommittal, infinitesimal nod, and wait for this supposed horrendous monster form of theirs to emerge.

Spylar closes their eyes, as if to concentrate on bringing his spider form out. Dark hair emerges, thick strands sprouting from their pores, covering their face, down their neck, and likely their whole body. A similar thing happens in my moth form, much finer yellow hairs appearing all over my skin. Two pairs of fuzzy spider legs sprout from his sides to give him eight limbs in total, if you include his arms and legs from his human form.

All my hairs are on end already at these changes, making them more spider-like. My spine tingles, and a tiny voice of fear blossoms in my skull, shouting *get the fuck out of here while you still can.*

On Spylar's face, fangs pop through their lips, two sets of them, larger than anything a vampire would have. From the sides of their face, two appendages grow out, resting around their neck like a draped garment, framed by their locs. I wonder what those are, not overly familiar with spider anatomy because why the would I be?

As if to drive the point home, Spylar slips off their jacket and pulls off their shirt, letting the four extra limbs which had sprouted spring outward unencumbered now. Sure enough, the dark hair covers his entire torso.

His eyes have multiplied, three more pairs smaller than the set centered on his face. They open, all eight of them completely topaz with no whites or pupils. Though Spylar is looking forward, they're not looking directly at me.

"And now you can see me as I truly am, in spider form."

Spylar does look like a spider. He's more spider-like than human now. My body is abuzz, and the tiny moth instinct voice is still shouting at me to run. Instead of listening to it, I get to my knees and move closer. Lifting a hand, I debate touching them. My hand is trembling. Am I that afraid? I put my hand back down.

"Are you afraid?" Spylar asks, as if it wasn't obvious enough already from my shaking.

They probably expected me to be scrambling away like a coward. I'm not, though. Maybe he thinks I'm scared stiff.

"Yes," I say. Spylar worries their lip with those large fangs which could probably tear into me like a dinner roll. "But I'm more scared that I find you more beautiful than frightening like this. I mean, not gonna lie, my instincts are fucking screaming at me. I'm not going anywhere, though. I'm not running away. I promise." My hand finds the courage to touch his cheek; the prickliness of their thin layer of facial hair is similar to the hairs on their fingers.

Spylar gives me a withering, tortured look. I'm ever captivated by his eyes. Now that there's eight of them, I'm captivated eight times over, and I might implode from it. "I don't want to hurt you." His voice is even more tortured.

"Then you won't. Have faith that whatever force draws us together will win over the animal part."

They nod. "I'll try."

"Do or do not. There is no try."

Spylar looks confused. "What?"

"Okay, adding Star Wars to the list."

"What's Star Wars?" They ask, and I can't help the laughter that bubbles up.

"A science fiction movie series. You really do live under a rock."

"Actually, I live in a treehouse, remember?" he says, deadpan.

"Do you....think you'll ever show me?"

"Perhaps. Would that please you?"

The smile that lights their face is like an irresistible open flame. I lose all fucking words, but I've gotta say something. "U-uhuh," is all I manage.

"Will you show me your moth form too?" They ask, and some sickening mix of thrills and chills turns my stomach.

He is entirely too irresistible like this, and I can't help wondering if I might be more irresistible to them when I change, too.

I nod infinitesimally and close my eyes, letting my moth form free. Some coaxing is required, as stirred up as I am. Unlike the first time when Spylar's spider pheromones scared it out of me, I've been around them more, and know how their presence feels. No accidental transformations have happened since the first one. Maybe he's also been holding back?

My yellow and red wings unfurl first. Much like stretching your arms after waking in the morning, it's a great feeling to let them free. I don't often transform. Mothmx usually only transform during the lantern festival or when mating with a fellow mothperson. Otherwise, we have no real reason to. Instead, we blend in with the humans, only recognizable to each other because of pheromones.

A light coating of yellow fuzz spreads over my arms, while my matching antennae sprout from my head. When I open my eyes, they are all red, whites disappearing in this form.

My antennae shudder as I take in Spylar taking me in. The first breath I take in full moth form turns into a gasp, followed by a whispered, "Fuck."

Just when I thought Spylar couldn't be any more appealing. Their earthy smell is intensified, and something akin to campfire smoke that I find so irresistible my mouth is practically watering. He's more appealing than an open flame or a lantern in the dark.

"Beautiful," he says, all whisper and wispy-voiced. Spylar lifts one hand, pausing in-between us. The air in the breath's width between our faces almost crackles with electricity. "Can I touch them?"

I nod in assent. Their hand closes the gap, prickly fingers running down the soft and delicate, sensitive surface of my wings. My whole existence narrows to the pads of their fingers and the electric feeling of the prickles moving, tracing along my wings, circling the black spot.

"F-fuck," I say on a gasp.

"You're exquisite," they say, voice lower yet still wispy, one side of their mouth quirking upward, no doubt in amusement at my swearing.

"You're dazzling," I reply.

"Could I um...try..." He licks his lips and glances down at mine, and I know what the end of his sentence should be without question.

If simple touches cause such static electricity, such intensity for us, what might a more intimate meeting of lips, or our bodies do? My whole being is on fire just at the thought.

"Y-Yeah," I squeak out, to my dismay.

"Stay still," they whisper, placing one hand as lightly as moth's wings upon my cheek. "Stay calm."

Even in my dazed and dazzled state, the similarity to the scene in the first Twilight movie isn't lost on me. It'd be lost on Spylar, though. The kiss is completely different in the book; Edward doesn't even say stay still. The meadow scene and the very domestic aftermath are sadly missing from the film.

Spylar's head tilts as he draws closer. Our lips brush, the beginning of a kiss, and that first spark of fire ignites within me. Whatever chemical reaction there is between us, I'm already about to lose my head over it. Their lips press fully against mine, and it's like going up in flames. How the fuck am I supposed to remain calm when it's like I'm errupting, the fire within me boiling over?

I press my lips back with zero grace and absolutely no calm. I'm anything but collected. A pathetic moan escapes my lips, and Spylar's tongue darts out to trace my lower lip, leaving a trail of searing heat in its wake. I respond in kind, meeting tongues with them and grasping into the back of their head, onto their locs, as if to lock him in place. As if he wanted to get away. As if I needed to entrap him. In truth, I'm the one who is at risk of being trapped. As if I could resist him. As if I could outrun him.

It's too late for me to save myself. All I can do now is cling to Spylar, simultaneously my demise and my desire, and hope his desire for company outweighs the desire to consume.

His extra appendages wrap around me, and now I'm the one entrapped. There's no escaping now. My mind is screaming at me, flipping back and forth between amorous and anguishing thoughts, pleasure and pain, flight or fuck. Their mouth and tongue are a hot brand on my own, their hands clutching at my shirt and their extra appendages clinging to me desperately. It's like I'm literally on fire at every place we're touching.

I trace my hands over his neck as my tongue dances with his own, bringing them around and sliding them along the two strange and smaller appendages which fall around each side of his neck, wondering again what exactly they are—perhaps fangs? Spylar makes a noise between a gasp and a moan, jerking away and leaping back suddenly. They land several feet away from me, crouching, both human arms and extra four spider arms straight and tensed against the ground, all eight eyes wide.

"S-Sorry. Did I do something wrong? Should I not touch those... whatever they are?"

Their tense face softens after a moment. "My pedipalps."

"What are pedipalps?"

Spylar chews their lip. "Um. My...reproductive organs."

"Wait..." I go wide eyed. "Like, your dick? Dicks?" Dicks. Plural. Spylar has two dicks... By his head.

Spylar nods. "To put it informally, yes. My dicks. Well, the spider equivalent of them, anyways. Spiders have palps instead."

My face is so hot I think I might be able to fry a fucking egg on it. "Holy fuck, I'm so sorry. I-I didn't know. I won't touch them again unless you ask me to."

"It's my mistake. I should've warned you." He pauses, smiling. "It wasn't unwanted, though. I wouldn't mind it at all if you wanted to touch them again. You just surprised me."

I'm still hung up on the realization of Spylar's multiple dicks—I mean palps—let alone the fact that they might want me to touch organs in question. My curiosity catches up quickly, though.

"How um... Does that work? During sex, I mean."

"I can use them on my partner by kneeling before them. Or, I can relocate them to my abdomen, for a more human-like experience."

I let that sink in for a second. Spylar can detach and reattach his palps to his body? Fuck me. The idea is both strange yet intriguing, weird yet arousing.

Spylar gets to his feet, staring at me with puzzlement. "So, have I managed to scare you off?"

I shake my head. "Not at all." I lift a hand out to him. "Will you come back over here?"

Spylar nods and approaches, kneeling before me and taking my hand. The prickliness of their fingers is getting more familiar to me, bordering on pleasant now. As frightening as Spylar is and should be to me, he's also devastatingly beautiful and intriguing.

About three things I'm absolutely positive. First, Spylar is a spiderperson. Second, there's part of them—and I don't know how potent that part might be—that desires to fill my body with their venom and suck the juices of my organs from my body. And third, I am unconditionally and irrevocably in love with him.

My fate has been sealed.

When I tilt my head up and slightly to the side, Spylar leans in to resume the strange alchemy of kissing.

Chapter Eight

Confessions

I'm not quite certain how long I spend just kissing Spylar. I feel like I'm dying. I feel like I've never been more alive, more real than in this moment, lip locked with my natural enemy, drinking in the taste and smell and feel of him.

Spylar urges me down into the grass with a gentleness so tender for a person made of such terrifying parts. They hesitate over me, bottom lip caught between their teeth.

"Is-Is that okay? With your wings out."

"Yeah, they're fine." I hold my arms open. "Get down here."

A shy smile blooms over his face, and Spylar obeys, lying down on me and nuzzling their face into the crook of my neck, smelling me and shuddering as they take that scent in, a scent which I have no doubt is equal parts appetizing and arousing to them, as equally as they are terrifying and tantalizing to me. I let my hands wander carefully down their arms. In his spider form, the prickly hairs cover their body. On their arms, they're longer, softer before ending in the odd, prickly tips. It's not unpleasant, not as much as his hands were to me at first.

"You smell so delectable," Spylar murmurs into my ear, giving me goosebumps.

"What do I smell like to you?" I wonder if he might say floral, though he's not to that chapter yet, it's the next one, and I wouldn't like it if I did still smell floral after transitioning. I'd hope I smell like something more manly. I'm not sure what, though. Sweat? Musky? Yeah, that, I guess. Musky.

"Hm... Like stone, and earth, and fire."

The things they list aren't smells, really. Stone and fire at least don't have a smell. And earth, maybe he means like the grass or dirt?

"I smell like dirt and smoke?" I ask aloud as I puzzle through their strange choice of words.

Spylar half laughs into my neck. "I apologize. I'm not good at describing human scents. I suppose it's a bit different for me." They lift their head to look at me, face soft and full of affection. "I promise, they are all pleasant scents, which I love. You smell like nature. Like home."

I smile. "Okay, good."

They bring a hand up to trace their fingers over my cheek, prickly side against my fuzz this time. It's less prickly with my fuzz in the way, and my face heats and my heart races at the touch, more bold than before.

"What about me?"

I struggle to form a reply. "Like pine... And wet moss... And. I don't know what else, but something I can't resist." That last one is probably the pheromones they put off which attract prey, attract *moths*.

"Mm," Spylar replies, smiling dreamily and dazedly, seemingly pleased with that response. He leans in and kisses the corner of my lip, and my chin, and my jaw. Everywhere but exactly on the mouth. Teasing. They're teasing me. Playing with me.

"You shouldn't play with your food," I say, a half-hearted jest.

I can't take this. My heart is beating wildly in my chest, and my pulse is racing. Whimpering, I tilt my head and capture their lips. Spylar hums in approval, pressing their lips to mine and tracing one finger lightly and gracefully as a spider over their web down, down, down one of my wings. I tremble and my antennae twitch.

Fuck, no one has ever touched me like that, so tortured and tender at once, and so, so gently, reverently.

Their additional appendages brace them on each side of me. One leg joins their hand in the reverent petting of my wings, and if this is too much now, what will I do when we possibly do *other* things?

I can't even imagine the depths of how my mind will be blown.

"Was...was that all right?" They ask, hesitance in their voice.

"Fuck, yeah. More than all right."

Spylar chuckles, a light and wispy sound Iike silk filling my ears. I could listen to that laugh forever. How easily I've already fallen into this rhythm with them, how quickly I'm getting used to his touch and his presence. I mean, I'll probably always be dazzled, but his touch is not unpleasant as it first was, and even though my heart still pounds with that mix of fear and excitement, I know Spylar won't hurt me.

A drop plunks my face, followed by another, and another.

"Aw, noooo."

Rain. Classic Forks.

We untangle and run to the cover of the nearest tree, transforming back to our human forms as we go. Spylar pulls their shirt back on and takes my hand. The prickles of their fingers brush between my knuckles, even more pleasant than before, shooting a delightful zing up my arm, though I also get goosebumps.

He lifts my hand, looking at me questioningly. "Is this all right?"

"Y-Yeah."

Spylar smiles, lifting my hand to his mouth and kissing my knuckles. "What now?"

Too dazzled for a second, I stare at them, dazed by those fire eyes. I swallow hard and try to clear my head.

"Um. I don't want to say goodbye to you yet."

"Then don't," they say, and kiss my hand again.

"Would you, uh..." Mothman, he's so fucking dazzling. "Wanna go grab a bite to eat? We could go to my apartment after and chill. If you like."

Spylar smiles warmly. "That would be great."

I pull the hood up on my jacket and we walk hand in hand back through the forest. Much like Edward and Bella, we're practically inseparable already. Just heading back to my place, not wanting to say goodbye.

"So, how many times have you compared us to Edward and Bella?"

It's like Spylar can read my mind. Just like Edward.

Damn it. I just did it again.

"An embarrassing number of times," I mumble, refusing to look at them.

"You don't have to be embarrassed," Spylar says, squeezing my hand. "I think it's cute."

"Is that code for you actually think I'm weird and creepy?" After all, there's no way he could find me or my strange hyperfixation on this cute in any way.

"Cal, you're not weird, or creepy." They stop and move in front of me, taking my other hand and holding them both tightly. The prickles send ripples through my arms. "If anything, I'm the creepy one. I live in the woods. And I've avoided and spied on you while you worked. Also, you're no weirder than me, being that I'm a spiderperson, and you're a mothperson. If anything..." He pauses, lifting each of my hands and kissing them like a perfect, princely being out of a fairy tale, and my heart races. "You can understand me better than anyone ever could. If this book is part of the catalyst that helped bring you to me, then I could never find that weird or creepy."

They really are like some regnal forest fae, or something. I don't think I can fucking form words, and here Spylar is pouring their heart out to me. I gulp down the nervous moths flittering inside me.

"Really?" My completely not regal reply comes at last, and I kick myself inwardly for that being all I could manage.

"Yes. I find you cute," they say, and coming from their lips, I don't mind that word all too much. They kiss my cheek. "And kind." He kisses my other cheek. "And brave." Another kiss, this time my nose. "And charming."

All of those things? Really? I don't say really again. I'll look like an ass. I'm just not eloquent like he is.

Their hands release mine, moving up to stroke my cheeks. My face is hot and prickly. I pull their hands down and look away.

"Stop it," I grumble and step to the side.

"I'm only telling the truth, Cal. Usually compliments are met with a thank you." His voice drips with a hint of facetiousness, a crooked smile carving a crescent on one side of his mouth.

I touch my cheeks, as if that'd fucking cool my face down, and stifle a snarky comment about rose tinted lenses and pheromones or some shit.

"Thanks," I say instead, smiling shyly and taking his hand.

We arrive at my old yellow beetle and I grin, gesturing to it. "Here's my red truck."

"It's not a truck or red."

"Get in, smart ass."

On the main drag through town, I ask, "Do you come into town much anymore?"

"No reason to."

"You really just hang out in the woods and eat whatever you catch in your webs, huh?"

"Yes," they say.

I glance at them. Spylar stares straight ahead, face neutral.

"Didn't that get lonely?"

He shrugs, but his brows pinch together. "I'm not sure I realized how lonely it was until it wasn't."

He reaches over and touches my thigh. I grab his hand and thread our fingers, bringing his hand up to kiss it.

"You don't have to be lonely anymore."

They squeeze my hand. "Thank you, Cal."

I can't help smiling at him. I pull us into the parking lot of the burger place I've been eating at way too frequently.

"Have you ever been to this place?"

"No. Do you like it?"

"Yeah, it's pretty good. Do you still eat normal food?"

It's strange asking such a question for me, since mothpeople eat like regular humans. They seem to have better reflexes and heightened abilities in their spider form, too. Hunter's reflexes. Mothpeople are just people with moth-like features, basically. Such a strange, weird world we live in, and such a coincidence these two lifeforms which humans have no fucking clue about might meet in the woods and perceive each other, maybe fall in love, and kiss. What a fucking wonderful world.

"Not too often. I prefer more liquid based foods, like smoothies or protein drinks."

"What about milkshakes?"

"Milkshakes are good," he says with a smile.

When we get out of my car, Spylar comes to my side and puts his arm around me, and we walk together to the burger place.

We get in line, Spylar's arm still around me, holding me closer. I lean against him and close my eyes for a moment.

"What do you usually get?" they ask.

"A burger and a shit ton of fries."

"Cal?" A familiar voice says. "And Spylar?"

My eyes snap open. "Jim." I tense up, and Spylar's arm does so too, but remains around me as a very confused Jim assesses us.

"You and Itamin, huh? Now that's a strange turn of events. How'd that happen? I thought you moved away, Spylar."

"I just don't live in town anymore," Spylar says, all mannerly, a half-truth.

Oh, this'll be a fun, fun watercooler conversation with Jim on Monday. Awk~ward.

Jim looks between us a couple of times, and at Spylar's fucking *arm* around me, and I can practically see the gears moving in his head as he figures out what this is, exactly. The second he does, his brows raise.

"How'd you two meet?"

"On the trail," I answer first, because who knows what Spylar might say. "I guess they still do some hiking, and I bumped into them."

Hopefully, Spylar picks up on the fact that I didn't say anything about moth stuff and takes the hint that it's a no-no. Mothmx have an understanding. We know not to tell humans anything. How it is for spiderpeople, I have no clue. As solitary as they are, it could go either way. Though, Jim didn't seem to know about Spylar's true nature, so I *think* it's safe to assume my secret's safe with them.

"Wow." Jim looks like he doesn't have a clue what to think. He looks over me, then over Spy, and to me again. "You look good, Spylar. Little more...peaky. But good."

"Thank you," Spylar says, cordial as ever.

"Well, I'll leave you two. Uh. Have fun?"

"See ya," I say, dreading that imminent see ya in reality.

"Nice seeing you again, Jim," Spy says.

"You too?" Not sure why Jim said that like a question, but okay...

He takes a couple steps back, lifts his hand in a lazy wave, and at last turns to leave the burger joint. Thank Mothman. I moan and bury my head against Spylar's chest, embarrassed as all out and knowing the embarrassment isn't over. I'm more than ready for it to be over.

"What's wrong?"

"Embarrassing," I grumble.

"Why?" Spylar laughs, whisper soft like moth's wings against my forehead, though their laugh is more of a hshshs than a hahaha.

"Because it's embarrassing. Jim saw us. Don't you care?" I glance up at them. Spylar's ember eyes just gaze at me with nothing but laid back warmth.

"No. I don't care who sees us."

My face is burning. Holy mothballs, why does he make me this way?

"Are you ready to order?" I blurt.

"Sure." Spylar smiles, kisses my forehead, and steps up to the counter with me.

I order for us, a burger and a shit ton of fries and two milkshakes. Spylar holds it all in their lap as we zip over to my apartment, which takes like, no time, because Forks is so tiny. We don't even have time for a conversation.

About all we manage is, "So, you're embarrassed easily?" from Spylar, and a "Shut up," with a hot face from me.

I fumble with the key to my door and let us in.

"So, this is my place..."

Spylar follows me in and looks around, at my plain walls and big couch with my purple blanket, and my TV, and smiles.

"It's nice and quaint," they say, earnestly, without a hint of sarcasm dripping in their voice, and my heart warms.

"Glad you think so. I was worried, since it's a little sparse. Moving across the country and all, you know."

"Ah." Spylar glances around, as if looking for something, maybe a dining table (which I don't have), then goes to the middle of the living room and plops down with our stuff. "I don't mind it. I'm not a person of many possessions myself, as you can probably imagine."

I sit across from him, remove our sandwiches from the bag, then rip the bag open to act as a plate for our fries.

"Oh, that makes sense. I was worried for nothing, then."

We both smile, and I take a sip of my milkshake before digging into some fries. I watch Spylar, as inconspicuous as possible, and they do the same, nibbling on fries here and there, taking long sips from their milkshake. I wonder if I might ever see him eat something other than human food. I wonder if I even want to. Suppressing a shudder, I shove that thought away. Probably not.

"We could watch something from the bucket list, if you want. Probably not Twilight yet, since you're not done with the book. We'll wait on that. Spider-Man? Batman? What sounds good?"

"Perhaps Spider-Man? I'm very curious to know what this Spider-Man is like."

I chuckle. "Okay."

We snuggle up on my couch after eating and watch the original Spider-Man movie, with Tobey Maguire, and it's so perfectly domestic that my heart might burst.

I think I've fallen for you, I don't say. *I think I'm in love with you*, I want to say. *I think I fucking love you*, I don't say.

"What'd you think?" I ask as the credits roll.

"It was pretty good. A bit preposterous, but interesting." Spylar looks contemplative, brows furrowing for a moment in a way that's much too serious for a superhero movie discussion. "I have a few questions, though. How did he get such a good looking costume all on his own? How do the webs shoot through it? And why do they even come from his hands?"

Oh. My. Mothman.

I can't help it, I'm cracking up. Clutching my belly, I fear my food might come up if I don't recover soon.

"Haven't... Haven't you heard... Of suspension of... disbelief?" I wheeze out.

"No? Is what I said that funny?"

I finally compose myself. "Sorry, I know you're not used to movies. It took me off guard, is all," I say, touching his leg and rubbing it lightly to reassure him. "So, you know how you accepted the premise that in the fictional version of our world established in Twilight, vampires exist? That's suspension of disbelief. Setting aside those unlikely things for a time and just accepting them for the sake of enjoyment."

"Oh. That makes sense, I suppose. So, I'm supposed to accept some of the things I don't understand for the sake of entertainment?"

I lean closer, smiling wide. "Exactly." Their breath reaches my nostrils a second later and sends me into intoxication, dizzying and wonderful. "Don't go," I say, quieter.

He moves infinitesimally closer, lips brushing mine ever so slightly in a way that's even more dizzying and torturous. I close the gap, quickly, before I can lose my nerve in the haze of Spylar's unconscious dazzling. Spylar immediately responds to the kiss, pressing their lips against mine firmly and bringing their hands to my cheeks, unabashedly running his fingers down my cheeks with the prickly side this time. It's electric, hot, and cold all at once.

After only a moment, Spylar breaks the kiss and stares at me with those fire eyes. They don't look as intense as usual, but hesitant.

"You want me to stay?"

They start to turn their head away, to avert their gaze, and I reach out to touch his cheeks now.

"Yeah." Their brows raise. My face heats. "Just to stay the night. Not um..."

Spylar smiles. "I'd like that. I don't want to go, either."

"Good." I take his hand and lead him into my bedroom. "Um. Do you want some pajamas, or something?" Come on, don't make it awkward, Cal.

"I'm fine, thanks." Spylar pulls off their pants, keeping their boxer shorts and t-shirt on. I try not to gape at their legs, forcing myself to turn away and pull off my pants, too, so now we match.

I slip under my purple comforter and hold it open, waiting for him to join me. He does, with a heart-melting smile more enticing than an open flame. Strong arms wrap around me and my body joins my heart, melting into them, so, so easily. As if I had any choice. Spylar is my flame, and I'm drawn to him.

"Oh, I get the reference now." I'm already headed towards dreamland when he speaks.

"Hm?" I don't bother opening my eyes or looking up at them.

"Bitten by a radioactive spider. It was a Spider-Man reference."

I snort. "Yeah."

"What's Kryptonite, though?"

"Different superhero called Superman. I'll add it to the bucket list."

"Oh. Okay. Goodnight, Cal." Spylar kisses the top of my head.

"Goodnight."

I fall asleep wrapped in their warmth, surrounded by their scent, safe and sound. Despite what the nagging part of my brain says.

Chapter Nine

The Treehouse

In the morning when I wake up, I'm still in Spylar's arms, and I'm greeted by their gentle breathing and intoxicating scent. It makes me want to lie here forever.

Forever will have to wait, I guess, because Spylar begins stirring. I nuzzle deeper into his chest, hoping maybe he'll just stay like this a bit longer.

"Good morning," they say. No such luck. Oh well.

"Morning. Did you sleep okay?"

"Snug as a bug," he says with a smile, and I hold in a bubble of laughter.

We both slide out of bed, and Spylar follows me like a shadow as I put on coffee and stare blearily at the trickling, hot liquid.

"What's on the agenda today?" I ask. "Anything you'd like to do?"

"I was thinking you could come to my treehouse. Since I've seen your place now, it's only fair I show you mine."

I grin. "I'd love that."

"Good." Their warm returning smile lights a flame in my chest.

I tear my eyes away and pour us some coffee. "Cream or sugar?"

"No, black is good."

"Cool. I drink mine black too," I reply, and take a long swig of the too hot drink to coax me to life. It hits my gut like a bug zapper. "I'm going to clean up, if that's okay with you. You're welcome to use my bathroom, too. If you'd like."

"Thank you."

I soak in another look at Spylar, who's brilliant even with bed head and sleep raggled, before disappearing into my bathroom to shower. I don't soak in the hot water for long, my belly abuzz with fluttering moth's wings at the idea of seeing Spylar's treehouse. As soon as I'm dried off, I put on my testosterone cream and step out of the bathroom in my towel, slipping into the bedroom to get dressed while Spylar is in my living room area. I throw on a plaid shirt and jeans and go into the living room.

Spylar is on my couch, looking at nothing in particular while sipping coffee.

"Oh, you could've turned on the TV if you wanted to. I should've said that before."

He smiles as he looks at me. "It's fine. I don't have a TV at my place. No electricity."

"Oh. Right. Treehouse."

"Yes." They stand and set their cup on the kitchen counter. "I'll freshen up, then we can go."

"Okay, great."

I fry some eggs while Spylar's using my bathroom, using my shampoo or whatever fucking else they want. God, it's so domestic. My heart is all warm and aflutter. It all seems so easy, now that we're headed down this path. I already can't bear the thought of him being away from me or out of my sight for long.

When Spylar reemerges, locs slightly damp, I'm unable to help gawking.

"Um. I made eggs. I also have cereal, if you want. Or I could make you a protein shake?"

"Sure. A protein shake would be good."

We eat at my kitchen counter, me with eggs and a small bowl of cereal, Spylar with his shake. More domestic stuff, more mundane reenactments I'm certain we'll have a laugh about later.

"Why are you smiling?"

"You'll find out later," I say, face heating. "More Twilight parallels."

"Oh." Their brows furrow cutely. I resist the urge to press my finger between them to smooth his skin back down.

"Ready to go?"

"Yes."

I drive us to the usual trail I meet Spylar on. When we step out of the car, I look to them.

"Your turn to lead the way."

Spylar nods and takes my hand, leading me along the trail, deeper and deeper into the dank green forest. When the trail veers, they keep taking us straight, into the wilderness, into the unknown, into the deep recesses of the woods usually untouched by people. In this complete solitude, away from civilization, there would be no one to witness or come running to help, should Spylar decide now to give in to the desire to consume me instead. I have complete faith he won't do that, though. If he hadn't harmed me in my own apartment while we slept in each other's arms the whole night through, when my guard was completely down and I was helpless, then they wouldn't now.

I'm absolutely certain. Even if part of Spylar still has that inkling, that instinct dwelling under his skin telling him I'm a meal, they aren't going to act on it. We're in too deep now, too attached. There's no going back.

"Almost there," Spylar says.

The trees are more towering, more menacing and thick and green in this deep wilderness. We come around a gargantuan tree trunk, and Spylar stops. Ahead, there's another behemoth of a tree, only this one has a structure cocooned into its trunk, bits of a house-like structure steepling from it. A half roof here, a window there, and a ladder up to a door that rests within one of the natural hollow maws of the trunk. There's another maw which is fashioned into a window, complete with a criss-cross pane and a curtain.

"Wow. It's literally a tree...house."

"What do you mean?" Spylar looks my way, head and one brow quirked.

"Have you never seen a typical treehouse?"

They stare, unwavering in their bafflement. Apparently not. "A typical, human treehouse is like, built up higher, around the branches and stuff. Rather than like, utilizing the structure of the tree itself in its structure to create one cohesive thing from two separate things, like your treehouse."

"Huh. That sounds terribly wasteful and illogical to me."

I hold back a laugh. "I guess it is. Humans are weirder than us sometimes, aren't they?"

"Yes. One of the reasons I decided to leave my job at the forestry department was because I have so much trouble fitting in within human society. While it allowed for a great deal of nature time, having to go into town every day and interact with even a couple people here or there was difficult for me."

I squeeze his hand. "Do you find it hard with me?"

Their brows turn upward, eyes catching the light in that way only a spider's cute little eyes do, and it's too fucking endearing.

"I enjoy your presence and company. I do worry, though, that I'm too.. Too... Boring?"

I grab their other hand and turn him to face me, clasping their hands tightly. "You're the most interesting person I've ever met. Especially for someone who just lives in the woods," I say, grinning.

The smile that lights their face is warmer than any open flame.

"Now, are you gonna show me the inside of your badass tree-in-a-house or not?"

"Yes, of course."

Spylar ascends the ladder first, opening the door and holding it open for me. It's rounded, molded to fit perfectly in the hole of the tree.

"It kinda reminds me of a hobbit hole."

"A what?"

"Another book series and movies for the bucket list." I take their offered hand and step through the threshold, into the den of the spider.

Most of the inner structure of the tree is intact, wood melting downwards with moss in some spaces. The floor is hardwood slabs, with a thick woven carpet of vines in the middle. Nestled into one alcove and taking up most of the space is a hammock of thick webs, likely handspun by Spylar themself. Fuzzy fleece blankets and some pillows are scattered in the web hammock. Vines hang around the entire space. Two small LED lanterns shine light dimly throughout the treehouse. Other than the hammock, there's a shelf with a few plants, books, and wooden figurines, and a small dresser, both of which look hand carved.

"How do you like it?"

"It's very cozy. Did you make the shelf and dresser yourself?"

"Yes."

I step closer to examine the items on the shelf. The books are all non-fiction, forestry and nature related. The wooden figurines are of animals: a deer, a bird, insects. The last one I lay eyes on is a moth, an io moth like me, I think. It's incomplete; only one side has the dots carved into the wings.

"Did you make these?" I pick up the io moth carefully, turning towards Spylar. Crimson blooms faintly on their cheeks. "Is this one supposed to be based on me?"

They nod, crimson darkening, eyes averting mine. I set it back down and move to stand in front of them, touching their cheek.

"You're extraordinary, Spy."

He glances up, face still hesitant and bashful. "I wouldn't say that. I'm a very simple creature who lives a simple existence."

"Did you build this whole house yourself?" They nod. "Then you really are fucking amazing, Spy. Most people can't even build a store bought shelf. So, accept my compliment."

A firelight of a smile ignites upon their face. "Thank you, Cal."

"I'm just being honest." I stroke their cheek and smile back at them.

Spylar reaches a hand up to stroke my cheek, too, the prickles on their fingers grazing over my flesh like moth-wing kisses. I think the prickliness is hardly bothering me at all, now. It's become almost pleasant, even. He leans in and presses a gentle kiss to my lips, painfully gentle, as if he's afraid he might fucking break me.

I guess Spylar still could yet break me. Not intentionally, but they could. Still, I refuse to give in to fear. I have to hold on to the hope that Spylar's affections for me will win over their instincts, and they'll be able to maintain control.

I press my lips against Spylar's, much less gently and far more ungracefully. At my core, I'm only a moth, after all. Tragically fleeting, and attracted to things that could burn and destroy me. We only have this one life, though, and there is no forever or guarantee of happily ever after, either.

The moth is ever fleeting in the presence of imminent death. But such is life for all beings, on different scales. Spylar may outlive me, or I him, but all we can concern ourselves with is the now. And I'm not going to waste a single moment of our little patch of paradise. I plan to spend as much time with them as humanly, mothly, spiderly possible.

"Would you like to relax on the hammock?" Spylar asks after moment of kissing back.

"S-Sure," I blurt, still heady from his kiss.

They climb into the hammock and hold a hand out for me, pulling me into their arms. Two more sets of arms join his human ones a few seconds later, and their chin is now bristly in that spidery way. It's heaven, despite the inkling at the back of my head saying I'm condemning myself to hell. That irksome instinct is waning more and more, and I'm beginning to feel...safe. At home.

We lie there for an indeterminate amount of time, Spylar's hands stroking lightly over my arms and back, lulling me to sleep. It's nice. After awhile, they pick up their copy of Twilight and we read together awhile. Spylar makes some notes and a couple of quips about us, and I'm red faced despite expecting the comments.

The rest of the day is spent this way, and on Sunday Spy comes back to my place and watches some more movies with me. He chose the 70s Superman.

Monday rolls around and I don't want to go to work. Why must capitalism be a thing? Why can't I blob under my blankets with my new spiderfriend?!

I'm not looking forward to seeing Jim, and the awkward conversation that will come with that, either.

"Can I run away into the woods with you?" I say into Spylar's chest.

"But who will look after the trees?" Spy replies, voice hissing with laughter.

"They're adults, I'm sure they're responsible enough to care for themselves."

Spylar laughs into my hair and pulls us up. "Go on, get ready for work. I'll be waiting for you when you come home."

"Promise?" I kneel on the bed and look at him.

"Promise," they say, pecking my lips.

When I step into the forestry office, the air of awkwardness immediately bares down on me like an anvil. Jim is pouring coffee in his Forks mug, and when he sees me, he looks at me too long and overfills it.

"Ah!" Jim hurriedly puts the pot back on the burner.

"Shit, Jim!" I rush over and grab paper towels to help clean the puddle of hot coffee from the floor.

"Sorry." He helps sop up the coffee and wipes his mug off, going to his desk and sitting there and sipping loudly and just *staring* at me.

"Do you have something to say?" I ask. mothballs, I just want him to stop gawking at me.

"You and Spylar..." he says after another awkwardly long and loud sip.

"Yeah... What about me and Spylar?" Don't tell me he has a problem with me being queer *now* of all times, now that I'm seeing someone. Someone he knows.

"Nothing. Nothing. I mean I'm happy for you, really. Always worried about that Spylar... He seemed a little...disconnected, I guess?"

Disconnected is an understatement.

Jim continues, "It was kinda weird seeing you together. But I think you might be good for them." He smiles warmly.

Oh. I'm not sure what to say. "Uh, thanks?"

He laughs lightly and relaxes more at last, leaning back in his chair. "They do look at you a little odd, though. Kinda like he wants to devour you, or something. I dunno."

He has *no* idea how apt that is. "In a bad way?"

"In an intense way, I guess? I'm happy for you, though."

"Thanks, Jim," I say, grinning and trying not to laugh. Thank Mothman he's not a bigot after all.

When I'm out surveying the forests surrounding campgrounds, I call up Jezz. I've been quiet and I need to tell her about Spy.

"Cal! I was beginning to wonder if you got lost in the woods!"

"No, just uh...busy. Sorry for going quiet on you."

"Water under the bridge, bro. How are you doing?"

"Good. Really good. I uh, met someone."

The squeal that comes through the phone is so piercing I have to hold it away from my ear.

"Oh my mothballs! Tell me everything! Gender? Human? Are you being safe?"

My face heats. "Mothra, Jezz. One thing at a time."

"Sorry, I can't help it, I'm excited for you!"

I tell her everything. Well, except for the stuff about spiderperson anatomy. I'm *not* going there with my sister.

I text Mal afterwards and tell him I'm officially a thing with the spiderperson.

Malcolm S: pics or it didn't happen

I reply with the emoji of a hand flipping the bird.

Malcolm S: happy for you, man

Me: don't go getting sappy on me now, gross

I'm smiling despite my reply.

We're in Spylar's treehouse tonight, which I'm pleased to say has collected more fiction books in the past few weeks, and some souvenirs from a Twilight gift shop in town I convinced them to go in with me. Spy's kissing me in that light yet devastinging way for theirs that leaves me dizzy and weightless.

I've spent every moment I can with Spy since that first night they came home with me. Sometimes we stay at my place and watch TV, sometimes at their place and read by lamplight. He finished the first Twilight book, and we watched the movie, and he had a field day with that one, holy mothballs.

I dip my hands beneath his shirt, capturing that topaz gaze with a brief, questioning look. "Can I take this off?" It's the first time I've asked to do it. Spy takes it off often at night, to let their extra legs free.

Spylar nods their assent, letting me pull their shirt off. Tossing it aside, I admire his taupe-skinned chest, strong yet graceful. The spider is ever deadly, yet full of grace and beauty. The fine fur blooms across their skin as my hands trace over their body. Their extra legs come out from their sides, curling delicately around me and imprisoning me in their sweet embrace.

I should feel like I'm in a trap. Instead I feel like I'm home.

They kiss me again, less tender, fangs teasing over my lower lip while two fuzzy spider legs slip up my shirt to caress my skin, leaving behind trails of goosebumps in their wake.

"Can I take yours off, too?" Spy asks, and my stomach swoops.

"Yeah," I whisper.

The legs pull my shirt up cleverly, Spylar's lips leaving mine for only an instant to pull it over my head before resuming the kiss. Their four arachnid legs enclose me, tracing the lines of my back while their hands roam down my sides, thumbs hooking on my belt loops.

That's when my body loses control and my moth form takes flight, orange-gold fur spreading over my skin as my wings and antennae emerge from my body. My brain catches up a moment later, taking in the realization that this is happening.

We've barely even started whatever this is.. I have no clue what to expect out of sex with a spiderperson. Outside of Sunil, which was before I'd transitioned, I've had no other sexual relationships or encounters. With him, it'd been all discomfort and more about him than me. I only ever did those things with him because I thought it was expected of me to fit into the disgusting cisgender heterosexual role that my parents had thrust upon me.

But I don't want to think of that anymore. I want now, with Spylar, whatever that entails.

I grasp for their pants, too, clumsily in my intoxicated state, heady from their kiss and their touch. Those four legs around me stand my hairs on end, creep tingles down my spine, and have my wings flittering helplessly, as if caught in the bowl of a lamp. And yet, Spylar's touches, light as spider's legs, Spylar's kisses, so criminally gentle, have my heart racing for an opposing reason. These opposing forces within my heart and head are so brilliant, so torturous.

We manage to undo each other's pants, despite the clumsiness and headiness we cause each other. I push Spylar's down. He does the same to mine, along with my boxers. Spylar has no underwear to speak of. Maybe there's no reason to with nothing in that area?

I glance downward to the space between their legs. Their light coat of fur covers their lower body, too. A thin slit, barely visible beneath the hair, is centered where genitals on most humans and humanoids would be. I wonder what that is... Maybe where their webs come out?

"Huh. I'm not sure what I expected. You did tell me about the..."

"Pedipalps." Spylar fills in the last word for me.

"Right."

I kick my shoes and clothes the rest of the way off. A moment of uncertainty skitters through me at the thought of what Spylar might think of my body, completely bared before them now, top scars and post-transition and all. Though, my chest hadn't been large, so I was able to get away with only incisions around my nipples. For my genitals, however...

Something different happens for mothpeople who transition. While a typical human transitioning from female to male can expect enlargement of the clit, the effects on mothpeople are... more prominent. It's like I actually have a dick, but with all the sensitivity of a clit. Yeah, it's a fucking experience.

Spylar's hands have paused, hovering over my chest. His brows are knit together, as if pondering or wanting to ask me something.

"Spy?"

"Yes?" They glance at me.

"Is um... Is everything okay? I mean... Do you like what you see?" Saying that makes me feel like a pathetic and insecure kid who's never done this before. In a way, I kind of am, since I haven't been in an intimate relationship since before my transition.

"Of course I do, Cal." They place a hand on my cheek. "How could I not love every part of the man I've come to love?"

Fuck, why'd he have to go and say that? Now I'm choked up. "You love me?"

"Yes. All of you." They stroke my cheek while their other hand splays itself over my heart.

I wrap my arms around the back of his neck and pull him closer, letting our bodies meld against one another.

"I love you, too, you know."

Spylar smiles. "I'm glad."

Our lips meet again. Spylar's extra legs hold onto my back, keep me melted against them, while their hands frame my face, stroking my cheeks.

"Cal? Is there anywhere off limits? Anywhere I shouldn't touch?"

"No. And um... I'm on a birth control pill, so you don't have to worry about that."

Spy takes this information in with a serious, considering face, followed by a lift of their brows and flush of cheeks, like they hadn't considered the vaginal penetration before this instant as a possibility.

"That's...good to know."

"Have... Have you ever done this, Spy?"

His flush turns deep crimson. Shit. "No... Have you?"

"Yeah, but before I transitioned."

Spylar's brows crease into each other again as he takes in this information. "Will you tell me if I do something wrong, or that you don't like?"

"Of course. And," I say, kissing their cheeks, then taking their hand from my chest and kissing that bristly palm and their fingertips as I continue between kisses. "Take... your...time."

Spy gasps as I kiss each digit, and their palps start twitching. I take one carefully in my hand and kiss the tip of it, too, earning a low *hsssh* from Spylar.

"Do you like this?" I ask, moving to kiss the other palp and move my hand along it in a gentle, slow, singular stroke.

"Y-Yeshsssh," they gasp out, the word half affirmation and half spider hiss. "But, I... I want to take it slow. So it'll be good for you..."

"It will be." I kiss the palp, moth wings light, before releasing it. "Take all the time you need. I'll be right here."

They cup my chin with one hand, prickly fingers spreading fright and delight over my skin like magic. Spy smiles and leans in to kiss me, slow and sweet, like savoring a sweet nectar. It's so reverent I might turn into a pile of goo within his gasp. Kissing truly is alchemy, capable of creating something inexplicable, something wonderful and more marvelous than the rarest gem. Kissing brings out the gold within the dirt, transforming a person entirely.

Suddenly, it's not simply you, it's *we*, and this thing between you which has been created, seemingly from nothing, yet it's been there all along. This curious and bizarre chemistry, under the right conditions, has gone through a mitosis to produce something new.

I can hardly think straight. I'm far past dazzled, utterly fucking razzled and rapt.

"Cal?" Spylar whispers in that hissy way of his against my lips, sending more shivers through my body.

"Y-Yeah?"

"Do you want to keep going?"

"You promise you aren't, like, going to try and eat me?" I wink, so hopefully they'll know I'm only kidding.

"Never," they say with a crooked grin, a light hssh hssh laugh bubbling from them as their eyes twinkle in amusement.

"Okay, then." I wrap my arms around the back of his neck again, touching noses with him. "I trust you."

Tangling my hands in his locs, I kiss him again, deeply and clinging to him as if my life depends on it. In a way, it does. Spylar is still more powerful than me, still the predator while I'm the prey. This could end badly at any moment, if they were to get carried away. This is the reason he always seems to be so gentle, I suspect.

Spylar is afraid of hurting me, afraid of going too far, so they feel like they have to hold back. Constantly restraining themself must be difficult. Hopefully, it's still worth it. Mothra, I hope so. I'm still not quite sure how this will work, if it'll work. But I want to try, Mothamn do I ever want to try.

As I kiss Spylar, delving my tongue deep and continuing to clutch onto them, I can't help arching my hips against them, though I'm not sure that does anything for them like it does for me. My cock brushes against their fuzz, which is softer in this area, yet still slightly prickly. It's enough to have my cock's sensitive nerves all firing.

"S-Spy," I gasp out, shuddering as I debate continuing to rut against them.

I run my tongue over one of their fangs and nip their lip before pulling my head back enough to look at them. Their arms are braced on each side of me, and their entire body is completely still and ridgid. Those eight eyes are all half closed as they stare down at me with a heady look. Over their main pair of eyes, however, the brows are pinched together.

"Spy? Is everything okay?"

They nod infinitesimally. "I just... um.... I don't know what to do, or expect."

I stroke their cheek and give them a soft peck. "Hey, it's okay. We'll figure things out together."

"Okay." He smiles. "Your eyes are dazzling like this, by the way."

My face colors a hot crimson that might rival the red of my moth form eyes. "Thanks. Yours are always dazzling, by the way. They're four times as dazzling when you're like this."

Spylar's smile widens. "Thank you."

"So, uh... How might a spiderperson normally do things?"

"I could align my head with your hips, and use my palps..." Spylar pauses, ashen skin turning crimson. "As well as my mouth."

"Oh." My whole body is on fire thinking through this. Spylar could potentially use both palps and his mouth on me... all at the same time. Holy fucking mothballs, Batman.

"Would you like me to try that?"

A knot is lodged in my throat, so all I can do is nod. Spylar replies with their own nod, kissing my jawline and down my neck, lips as light as spider's legs crawling over my skin, leaving tiny pins of fire in their wake. Their lips pause on my neck, tongue running over my throat, right where an Adam's apple would be. Spylar laps at my neck, savoring as if partaking of a forbidden fruit.

They continue their trek downward, over my chest, over one nipple, and I gasp, hips bucking into the air, barely grazing fuzz.

"Spy?"

"Hm?" He doesn't pause his mouth, tracing his tongue around and exploring my nipple and the small half circle scar along the bottom of it. I bite back a gasp.

"Um... You can use both palps? At the same time?"

"Yes." Spy sucks on the nipple, slowly suctioning the bud into their mouth and sending shockwaves through my body.

"Ah... Um... Do you have something we could use—" Spylar moves to the other side of my chest and gives it the same treatment. It's almost as if they're playing with me. How fucking torturous of them. Do spiders torture and play with their food? "For lube?"

"Lube?" He lifts his head, looking at me questioningly.

"Some sort of salve, or lotion?"

"Oh. I have some aloe vera. Would that work?"

"Yeah."

Spylar rises from the bed and grabs a small jar from their shelf. They place it on the floor and kneel in front of the web. When their hands touch my legs, I scoot forward for them.

"Do you want me like this?" They ask.

"Y-Yes. Good." Their hands rest on my knees, and I spread my legs to grant them access. "What should I do with this?"

My face burns. "My front hole won't need any lubrication, but my other hole will. It'll need a bit of prep with your finger first."

"Okay." The jar opens, and a moment later Spylar's finger runs between my legs, downward until he finds my asshole. "H-Here?"

"Yeah."

He presses the slick finger in slowly, and I relax my body as it slips further and further in.

"Okay?" He asks.

"Yeah, it's fine. You can move it and work it for a bit."

Spylar moves their finger out and slowly back in. Soft, silky digits—their palps—slip around my waist, and their tongue strokes a line of fire up my swollen and neglected cock while they move their finger.

"Is this okay?"

"Y-Yes," I gasp. "Don't stop."

He keeps stroking his tongue up and down, up and down my cock while stroking his finger in and out, in and out of me, and fuck, I already feel like I might combust from it. My cock throbs and weeps a bead of cum.

"I'm ready," I say, even though I'm probably not. I can't fucking take it anymore. I can't wait anymore. I need to feel Spylar inside my holes and enveloping my cock, I need him everywhere all at once. "Use your palps now. Put some more aloe on the one you use in my ass."

Spylar removes the finger and strokes their palps along my inner thighs. He seems to have full and fluid movement of them, almost like two serpents slithering along my skin. The thought of those two digits penetrating me both at the same time is mind blowing, and I can't contain a shudder.

One palp, cool and slick, slides past the ring of my ass and partly inside. A second later the other joins in to penetrate my other hole. Both only just are inside, barely enough to feel them, yet my whole body might just explode from the anticipation. The palps slide in simultaneously, and I gasp as they move deeper and deeper inside me, filling both my holes to the brim.

Fuck. Fuck. Fuck.

"C-Cal... Is it okay?"

"Y-Yes. Spy, please... Please fuck me."

Spy grasps my hips, still with all the gentleness in the world, and their palps begin to move, slow movements out and back in, as if testing the waters first.

"A-Ah, please..." Fuck, it's so much. It's not enough. It's so fucking good. The fine coat of fur covering their palps is imperceptible to my asshole, but to the other... They're like a thousand little feelers stroking along my inner walls.

"Please what?" Spylar asks, almost a whisper, his S coming out as a hssh.

"More, more. Move more. Please."

Those palps are so pleasure inducing already, I've devolved into begging. It's a little pathetic, but I don't care. Spylar is obliging, moving in more of a rhythm now, palps bringing me tormenting ecstasy with each achingly slow movement in and out. I can feel them pressing against each other within me, striking my g-spot together. My body jolts, including my wings and antennae, and I moan loudly every time Spylar's palps hit that spot deep inside me.

Spylar's quiet gasps are smothered by my moans.

"Do...you...like it?" They ask between little pants.

"Fucking A, yes. Do you?"

"Yes," he says, gasping and wispy. "You feel so good inside, Cal."

I can only whimper in response, my antennae twitching and body trembling. "Y-You can... use your mouth, too..."

Spylar lowers their mouth down onto my swollen, needy cock, and holy fucking mothballs, it's a whole new level of pleasure, sending me from sky high to outer space. One thing I learned when I transitioned is how much more sensitive it can make everything. Between my own body and Spylar's palps, though, there are no fucking words for how amazing it feels.

My orgasm takes me within seconds of Spylar's mouth descending on me, spidering white-hot webs across my vision.

Tremors sling like Spider-Man webs through my body, my wings, my antennae. Holy fucking A, if Spider-Man had been anything like this Mary Jane would never leave him alone.

Spylar moans around my cock and increases the speed of his palps. I ride the waves of my orgasm until my body gives out and turns to jelly. Spylar's palps continue to work my holes, pleasure already building back up to another big O within a few moments. Spylar's tongue twirls about my cock, our moans and his hsshes filling the treehouse.

A whole new world of fucking ecstacy explodes within me when Spylar's palps begin to do this strange rotating thing. It feels fucking amazing, and it shoots me up to the edge of another orgasm within seconds.

The whirling movement intensifies, throwing me over the edge into an orgasm so fucking hard moans are more like screams. Spylar's palps press deeper, low, rumbling hiss-gasps coming from him as he shoots hot webs of come deep inside my holes. They suck my cock hard one last time before removing their mouth. A final shudder and moan escape me as one final web of my climax spiders through my body.

Spylar retracts their palps from me, deeper than I realized in the midst of our fuckfest. I shudder, and they press gentle kisses to my hips while stroking my trembling legs.

They look up at me, come seeping from their palps, dripping down in webs at the tips. It looks thicker, more web-like, with silken strands throughout. My lower parts throb, already aching for him again.

"Did you like it?" A questioning, insecure look crosses their face, and he looks away as he awaits my answer.

"Did I like it? Holy fucking mothballs on a skewer. Like would be a fucking understatement. You blew my fucking mind."

They smile, wide and warm, eight eyes brimming with joy. "Good."

"I don't think anyone else will ever satisfy me now that I've had spider sex."

Spylar gives me a crooked smile. "Never fear. No one else will have you. I don't plan on leaving you, my sweet mothman."

Shit, my heart's going wild in my chest. I love him so fucking much.

"I wanna cuddle you now. Let's clean up."

"As you wish," Spylar says, and I beam at him as I make a mental note to add The Princess Bride to our bucket list.

Chapter Ten

Occasions

I wake the next morning, entrapped in the web of Spylar's arms. Our naked bodies are tangled and crossed up like a web of spider legs and human legs. We're a web of limbs upon a web.

I'm absolutely certain Spylar won't kill me now. Not after last night's mind blowing.

Spylar stirs, a twitching of limbs and a half hssh, half yawn. They open their eyes and flash me a smitten smile that makes my heart race. They're still in their spider form, beady eyes bleary and endearing as a jumping spider.

"Good morning."

"Morning," I reply, heat suffusing my cheeks because he's just so fucking cute.

They lean in to kiss my neck, fangs grazing the skin playfully.

"You were amazing last night, by the way."

The way he can say such earnest and genuine things without a string of embarrassment shoots through my insides and melts me into a useless blob. Mothman, I love him.

"Y-You were, too," I stammer, because he's doing that thing where he dazzles me again.

Spylar's nibbling continues, their hands wandering over my chest while their arachnid legs trace goosebump inducing lines down my spine. Shivers web outward from their touches. Their head moves further down, a fang catching lightly on one nipple, and I gasp. Fuck. Heat pools between my legs, my cock throbbing as it swells.

I find enough will amidst my intoxicated state to touch Spylar in return, running my fingers down their firm and fur covered stomach. Touching their hips, I run my thumbs around them a moment before pausing.

"Um, Spy? Can I ask something... about your anatomy?"

Spylar's head lifts back up to mine, a warm smile on his face. Eight fiery eyes entrap me. "Of course. What would you like to know?"

I shove down embarrassment. My red face is a lost cause, though. "About this slit...." I trace a finger closer to it, not touching it, though, in case it's something they'd rather me not. "What is it?"

"Ah. My webs come from there."

"Oh." So, it's as I suspected. "Is it... Okay for me to touch there?"

"Yes," Spylar breathes out, a gasp, a hssh. "If you like."

I move my finger to trace along the fine slit. It gives willingly, like the folds between my own legs, like I could press my finger inside...

"Hssh," Spylar gasps out.

"I-I'm sorry." I pause. "Did I hurt you?"

"No. It's just... Very sensitive."

"In a good or bad way? Should I stop?" The last thing I want is to make Spy uncomfortable.

"Good," Spy gasps, lips against my ear, and I get goosebumps.

"Good?"

"Yes..." Their S comes out as a hiss, like a snake. It's cute and sexy at the same time, and I'm unable to help grinning.

Carefully, I run my finger along the web slit again, and it gives readily. Like, really readily. My finger easily slips in. Spy sucks in a sudden breath.

While my cock can get hard, it's not as rigid as a cisgender guy's, so I never thought about the possibility it could penetrate the tight channels of an ass, or even a cunt. Spylar's slit, though... I wonder.

"Spy, um... Can I ask something else?"

"Yes," they reply, hissy again.

"Is... Is penetration an option for your slit? Would...you be up for trying it?"

Spy glances at me with a lidded, heady face, and nods, almost infinitesimally.

"Can I ask one more thing?"

"Of course."

"You uh, mentioned being able to move the palps... I had an idea. Would you be able to move them down there now?"

"I could."

"Cool. Do you want to try it?" I try in vain to quell the heat in my face from the awkwardness of this conversation. Hopefully, it pays off. My body is on fire at the thought of it, of me penetrating Spylar while he plunges both his palps into me.

Spy considers this proposition with far more seriousness than your average person might, eight eyes narrowed in thought and face pensive for a long moment before their eyes finally widen, and they figure out where my line of questioning had been leading. I think.

Spylar nods, and I watch, intrigued, as they bring their hands to their face and easily detach the pair of palps. It's equal parts strange, unnerving, and sexy. I wonder if I should be weirded out or repelled, but I can't manage to be either. What does that say about me? I'm just as weird, I guess.

They bring the palps down to the space between their legs, reattaching them to two almost imperceptible, tiny slits beneath his web slit I hadn't noticed before. The palps pulse as they latch back into Spylar's body. So strange. So sexy. Fuck. My own cock and cunt twitch with anticipation.

I hook a leg around Spy's hip and pull them closer, half onto me, and kiss them. Spylar makes a muffled moan against my lips as our bodies press together, rolling into me. My skin hums and thrums, breaking out in goosebumps everywhere we touch, Spylar's fine hairs prickling my own, finer haired skin.

Spylar's kiss and touches consume my entire being. It's hard to do anything else except turn to liquid beneath them, as if they'd injected me with their venom and literally turned my insides to fluid.

"Cal... What would you like me to do?" Spy wisps in his hissy voice against my lips, electric webs shooting through me with each movement of his lips.

"I-I want you to fuck both my holes with your palps while I fuck your web hole," I blurt out, half the words sludging together.

Spylar's hips twitch, which I take for him liking my proposal. They sit up, fumbling around on the floor for a moment before returning to kneel between my legs, jar of aloe in one hand. As they slick their palps with the salve, I stare, agape and aroused as fuck.

When they shift closer, I lift my legs to wrap around his hips and pull him towards me. Spylar positions his palps at each of my holes and slips inside me, deeper and deeper, so much fucking deeper than when his palps were on his head.

"Oh, f-fuck, yes... Spy," I gasp, reaching between us and finding their web slit, lining up my cock, and pushing myself inside them.

My cock slips in quickly, and I gasp loudly, tightening my legs around him and bringing all the places we're connected as close as fucking possible. I stay completely still, taking it all in, and so does Spylar.

"F-fuck, S-Spy," I say, barely able to speak. "How does it feel to you?"

Spylar's hands find my cheeks as their spider appendages slip around my waist.

"A-amazing, Cal. You feel so amazing."

"So do you." I wrap my arms around them and squeeze them with my legs. "Wanna move?"

"Yesss," he hisses out, kissing me before the hiss stops. The sound fills my mouth, hot and thrumming as Spy begins to move their hips.

"Holy fucking mothballs, Spider-Man," I moan out, unable to keep myself from saying it aloud because, holy fuck I've never felt *anything* like this.

The feeling of their palps deep inside me and their slit wrapped around me like silk webs only intensifies when I arch my hips to meet them and thrust myself deeper inside the unexplored depths of them. I never expected this to work so well, for us to fit together so fucking perfectly. I'm afraid Spylar has spoiled me to anyone else now. He just feels so amazing. How will we ever stop?

"Cal, Cal," Spylar whimpers against the kiss, tightening his extra arms around me more, almost a vice grip, yet oddly gentle at the same time. I should feel trapped, doomed. I've never felt more free and alive.

I'm soaring rapidly towards climax between Spylar's palps and web hole all thrusting against me at the same time. Their slit, wrapped so gently around me, fitted so perfectly as if made for my trans mothman dick, coils around me like a million tiny threads of silken web caressing the million tiny nerve endings of my cock.

"Oh, fuck, fuck, fuck, Spy!" I cry out, climax taking me, shooting me from the sky and into space as I jolt and hold onto Spy for dear life.

Spylar's palps rotate in very gentle circles within me, their hips slowing to a lazy movement as my body trembles and rides out the orgasm.

"Good?" Spylar asks, capturing my eyes with his topaz ones in a questioning look.

"Fuck, yes, Spy."

I tremble and arch into him, and his pace quickens again, palps undulating inside me more rapidly while the inner workings of their slit do that mind blowing thing again that's like thousands of threads weaving around my come wet cock, as if enclosing it in webs.

Their spider limbs hold me tight, and their lips meet mine, and my whole being is consumed, my whole world narrowed to this moment and all the places we meld together as one. It's a Herculean effort not to come undone all over again, and so soon after my first orgasm.

Spylar's extra legs grasp mine and push them up more, touching my knees to my chest. My cock and their palps slip even deeper. Spylar trembles and makes a sound somewhere between a hssh and a whimper as my cock plunges further into them, and I think I might've found the spiderperson G-spot or prostate or something.

His movements are messy, erratic as we thrust, and I continue to hit that spot deep within them, which I swear I can feel, almost like a finger rubbing my sensitive cock. It only takes a couple moments, a few more movements of our bodies before we're both bursting, moaning into each other's mouths and kissing messily as we come. My wings twitch while Spylar's extra legs hold onto me desperately, as if squeezing the life out of me—or every last drop of come. I'm not sure which, or if it's both.

It's too much. It's not enough. It's too soon. I don't think I'll ever get enough.

Spy pulls out and turns us in our sides, holding me close as we both catch our breath.

"When... can we...do that again?" He asks, and I chuckle.

"Fuck...As soon as...we catch our breath."

Again and again, day after day, night after night. We'll read and watch all the things on our list, we'll hold each other and fuck each other. Every day with Spylar will be a special occasion which I'll treasure for the rest of our lives.

No measure of time will be enough, but we'll start with as close to forever as we can. We'll continue happily through our little bit of heaven we've carved out of life for as long as possible. And I wouldn't have it any other way.

Did you love *Spider Moth*? Then you should read *Moth Pit*[1] by Amara Lynn!

[2]

It all starts with a hum, a thrum, a bum bah dum dum.

Every year, the ultimate moth rave takes place in the mountains of West Virginia, unbeknownst to most people. To the community of mothpeople who do know about this moth pit, it's the best kept secret in the country.

For Erris, it's a burden.

With expectations of finding a mate, and Erris having little interest in romance, it's nothing but a tedious chore. Enter Sol, a friend from high school with social anxiety who also wishes

---

1. https://books2read.com/u/3RLdex

2. https://books2read.com/u/3RLdex

for the party to be over. Between the two of them, they might just have a chance at getting their hassling parents off their wings, and as an added bonus, the local toxic pest, Ren. All they have to do is pretend to be together.

Easy enough, right? Except in spending time together, Erris and Sol realize something real might be there after all.

Moth Pit is a 15,000 word contemporary fantasy new adult novella, and features mothpeople, a nonbinary/male romance, fake dating, and a friends to lovers arc. Cryptid and mothman lovers are welcome and encouraged!

Read more at https://amarajlynn.com/.

About the Author

Amara Lynn has always been a quiet daydreamer. Coming up with characters and worlds since childhood, Amara eventually found an outlet in writing. Amara loves anything to do with pirates, villains and superheroes, angels and demons. They were born and raised in the Midwest USA, where they remain stuck with their spouse and two cats. They love to write about soft monsters and cryptids, grumpy enbies, and forever will be weak for the grumpy one is soft for the sunshine one trope. When not writing, they are usually watching anime, playing games, and obsessing over their out of control music playlists.

Read more at https://amarajlynn.com/.